RIDING FOR THE BRAND

Sage Country

Book Three

By DAN ARNOLD

Books by Dan Arnold/Daniel Roland Banks

Fiction

Contemporary Detective

Angels & Imperfections   Special Agent   The Ticking Clock

Western

Bear Creek   Alta Vista   Riding For The Brand

Non Fiction

GUNSHOT WOUNDS
LEAVE PUCKERED SCARS
IF YOU LIVE LONG
ENOUGH FOR THEM TO
HEAL.

RIDING FOR THE BRAND

Sage Country

Book Three

By DAN ARNOLD

Much like that of the samurai who has pledged loyalty and service to his lord, the term "Riding for the brand", refers to a commitment, a responsibility and a sense of belonging.

Simply stated, to ride for the brand means to be loyal and faithful to the outfit you represent.

It is a code of honor.

LIFE IN BEAR CREEK ~ POLITICS AS USUAL

1.

My bullet wounds were healing nicely. At least the physical wounds were. I'd regained most of my strength and range of motion, but I was reliving some of the recent events in my dreams. Not really reliving them, but some distorted dream version of those events filled with dread and anxiety. I would wake Lora as I thrashed about, or even cried out in my sleep Sometimes I'd wake up reaching for my gun, or covered in a cold sweat.

Lora would hold me and soothe me like a small child, until I went back to sleep.

"This is no way for a man, let alone a lawman, to act. What's the matter with me?" I thought. *"I've been shot before, and didn't have these problems. Maybe I'm no good anymore."*

After a couple of weeks of misery, I finally admitted those thoughts to Lora. We were sitting on the porch, watching the kids playing in the yard.

"John, from what you've told me, your nightmares aren't really about you. You're concerned for our safety, me, Sarah and Jacob. You're feeling overwhelmed and vulnerable. It's not surprising. That horrible man walked into our bedroom and caught you naked and unarmed. You nearly died trying to protect me and the children. Anyone would be shaken up. I think about it too…sometimes."

I took a deep breath.

"Maybe, but what am I going to do about it?"

"Time heals all wounds," she quoted.

"Well, I reckon so, but how much time? I don't even want to leave the house. I'm afraid to be away from you and the children. At the same time, I need to get back to work. I know people are starting to talk."

"People have been talking about you since the first day you came to Bear Creek. Some people love you, some people hate you, and some people don't care one way or the other, but everybody talks. Those that hate you will try to take advantage of this situation and use it against you. They don't matter.

You matter. You matter to me and everyone in Alta Vista County. You matter to the children. Forget about the haters and focus on who you are, and what you do best."

"What I do best, is law enforcement."

Lora smiled and batted her eyes at me.

"Well, that's one of the things…"

I laughed.

It was the first time I could remember laughing, since being shot.

"I got a letter today from Mildred. She and Bud are coming back to Bear Creek, the end of next week," Lora said, changing the subject.

Bud was the pastor of our church and Mildred was his wife. They'd been gone for more than a month, called back east for a family emergency.

"That's good news. It will help get some things back to normal."

Lora was studying me.

"Do you remember when we were first engaged?" She asked.

"Of course, we're still newlyweds."

"Do you remember how I almost called off the engagement?"

"Yep, it worried me some, at the time."

"Do you remember why?"

I nodded slowly. I was beginning to get her drift.

"You were afraid something would happen to me, and you would be left alone."

"Do you remember what you told me?"

"I said fear and faith couldn't co-exist, I said they were like oil and water..."

Lora cupped my face in her hands and locked her eyes on mine.

5

"You were right, John. Faith and fear are complete opposites. I choose faith. I choose to believe God knows what He's doing. I have faith in Him, and I have faith in you." She kissed me. "And that's why I believe you're going to be just fine."

She stood up and smoothed out her dress. "Now, let's go play with the children."

It was true. Lora and I really were newlyweds. We were newlyweds with children.

Just before we were married, I found two kids, Jacob and Sarah, hiding in the livery stable. Sarah was four and Jacob was six. They'd walked barefoot, more than fifteen miles to Bear Creek, all alone. When I found them they'd been hiding in the barn at the livery stable for more than a week. Lora insisted they come live with us. At first they couldn't or wouldn't speak, but Lora had them eating out of her hand within days. We learned both of their parents were dead. Someone had killed their father, and their mother died of some sickness not long after.

We played with a wagon wheel rim and a stick for a while. Sarah was becoming more coordinated with the toy and could keep it up and moving now, but she still ran over things with it, or tripped on her skirts and used the opportunity to seek solace in the arms of Lora. Eventually, Lora went in to see about supper with Sarah following along right behind her.

I sat on the fence with Jacob, watching the carriage horses grazing in the pasture.

"Did you have horses at your place?" I asked.

Jacob nodded his head vigorously.

"Sure, my pa had a big old brown horse with a white face. His name was

7

Shongaloo. Pa rode him most of the time. We had a couple of giant horses to plow and pull the big wagon. We had a big wagon and a buckboard. We had other horses for the ranch too."

He and Sarah were becoming much more comfortable talking about their parents now. It had been a process over the weeks, but they were getting a little more open every day.

"I know you told me you had a milk cow. Did you have any other cattle?"

Jacob nodded again.

"A whole bunch, I don't know how many. My pa called it a herd. There was a big roundup every year where all the ranches caught all the cows on the range and counted them. Sometimes, other cowboys would help my dad round them up and do branding and such. I got to go out to the roundup a couple of times with Sarah and our Ma. It was noisy and messy but kind of fun. Burning hair stinks."

He was starting to look a little wistful, so I changed the subject.

"Do you think I should bring Dusty down here from the livery stable?" I was referring to my buckskin horse.

Jacob just shrugged.

"I think he likes living at the livery stable. It's pretty close to the courthouse, so I still see him every day, but I would rather have him here."

"If he was here, could I ride on him sometimes?" Jacob asked.

"I expect so."

"Well then, you'd probably better bring him on down here, huh?"

"You might be right, Jacob." I said, giving his hair a scrub with my hand. "You told me you lived near Yellow Butte. How close was it?"

"What do you mean?" He asked.

"I mean, could you see it from your house?"

"Course," he responded. He made a face indicating he had some concern about my intellect.

"You said you'd been up on the butte with your dad. Did it take a long time to get up there?"

He shrugged.

I tried a different approach.

"When you were up on Yellow Butte, could you see your house from way up there?

"Yep, right down below us. I was going to chunk a rock, but my pa said not to."

Now I had a much better idea about where they'd lived. I had the beginning of a plan forming in my mind.

10

"You know, we could play some baseball till supper time," I suggested.

Jacob smacked me on the leg as he jumped down from the fence.

"Tag, you're it" he called, racing away.

***

Down at the edge of Bear Creek, Lora and the children were having a fun time. From my vantage point in the dappled shade under a cottonwood tree, I was watching them splash water at each other, laughing and playing. I was delighted by their joy.

Looking toward the nearby hilltop, I saw a lone Comanche sitting on his pony. I wasn't disturbed seeing him, because I was pretty sure he was my friend, Yellow Horse. If it was Yellow Horse, I'd be glad to see him. With the sun behind him, I couldn't clearly distinguish his face. Other men on horseback

11

began to appear at the top of the hill, riding up from the far side. I felt uneasy.

There was something dark and menacing about these men whose shadows stretched out before them as they started riding down toward us.

Lora and the children had become silent. When I glanced toward them, they were looking up the hill at the approaching men on horseback. Those riders began to trot, then gallop down the hill.

They were close enough now I recognized them, but it couldn't be. These charging horsemen were all men I'd killed!

I called out to Lora, trying to warn her. She and the children were walking back toward where I was now standing out in the open meadow.

The riders were barreling down on them. I reached for my gun, but found myself standing in my long johns—undressed and unarmed. I felt frozen in place as the dead riders overtook Lora and the children.

DAN ARNOLD

2.

The next morning, we were all having breakfast in the Bon Ton Café, Tom, Becky, Jacob, Sarah, Lora and I.

I was thinking about what a short time ago I'd come into this city feeling all alone in the world. Now, I had a new wife, sort of a readymade family, and good friends. I was glad to be alive, and all too aware of how close I'd recently come to being dead.

"Are you OK, John?" Becky asked me.

"Oh, yes. I'm fine, just day dreaming, I expect."

"That's not surprising; I reckon you're entitled to be a little pre-occupied, John. It's been less than a month since you were shot." Tom said.

15

Tom is the Chief of Police in Bear Creek. Becky is his wife. They're expecting their first child.

Lora was watching me, looking a little worried.

"He hasn't been able to sleep very well. He has terrible nightmares, but he insists on getting back to work. He can't wait to get back in harness." She said.

"Crime rests for no man," I observed.

"John Everett Sage, you have more than enough deputies to manage the duties of the Sheriff's Department for at least another couple of weeks." Lora scolded.

I shook my head. "No, we're a little short staffed, what with Ed being up at North fork, and Bob having quit to find greener pastures."

"Lora is right. You should take another couple of weeks to recuperate, Tom

16

said, and then he lowered his voice. "Besides, it might not be a bad idea for you to be out of the limelight for a little while longer. Certain people are pretty upset about the shootout up in North Fork. There's talk you're just too uncivilized and dangerous to be the Sheriff of the county. All this attention in the press is not good for the city of Bear Creek."

"Is that how you feel?"

"Of course not, but that's not the point. John, there are people already looking to find a candidate to run against you. Some pretty influential people are saying it's time for a new Sheriff, right now. The sooner all this dies down the better..."

"Excuse me, Sheriff...?"

I nearly jumped. I hadn't even noticed the well-dressed man's approach.

It worried me some. People don't usually walk up on me without me seeing them coming.

"…My name is William Bartholomew Masterson. You may have heard of me. My friends call me 'Bat'. I've been a lawman myself. These days I'm a writer and sports promoter in Denver, and I was wondering if you would do an interview with me. You know, for the newspapers? I can get you the cover of the Police Gazette, and with my connections in New York City, I can get your story published all over the world." The man was rather energetic in his manner, and he had a big, toothy grin on his face.

Since the shooting, Bear Creek was full of newspaper people, tourists, people attracted to celebrity, and those intending to make a buck from all the excitement.

I'd even heard some low life types were selling fake replicas of items that may or may not have belonged to the famous outlaws who were killed up at North Fork.

Still, I was surprised Bat Masterson would bother with the story of the events. Masterson was well known as a man who always found his way to the most personally profitable enterprise, even if it was not entirely legal.

I intended to inform him I had no interest in having anything to do with the Police Gazette, a magazine arguably the most lurid publication in the country. It was typical Masterson would be involved with a publication of such low standards. He'd been regaled in the magazine as a great sportsman and gambler.

Still, out of courtesy, Tom and I both stood up to shake hands with the man.

"How do you do, Mr. Masterson? Of course we've heard of you. May I present my wife Lora, and the children, Jacob and Sarah. This is the Chief of Police here in Bear Creek, Tom Smith and his wife, Becky."

"I'm pleased to meet all of you. As I said, my friends call me Bat. I hope we'll all be friends."

He was a bit overdressed for a Saturday morning at the Bon Ton. He wore the latest and most stylish, dark grey suit, with a matching waistcoat, a white shirt with a celluloid collar, and a neck tie. His walking stick was his most notable affectation.

While he appeared to be freshly shaved, Masterson had a bushy mustache he was training to curl up on the ends.

He appeared to be a few years younger than me, and a little thicker through the waist.

In keeping with the local ordinance, no handgun was clearly in evidence.

"If you gentlemen will excuse us, I promised the children we would go shopping today, and now would seem like a good time." Lora said, as she stood and began to organize the children.

"I'll go with you, Lora. I've been meaning to have a look at the latest Sears Roebuck and Company catalogue. I'll bet I can make any item of children's clothing they sell, and do it right here in Bear Creek." Becky chimed in.

Both ladies were avoiding any acknowledgment of Mr. Masterson.

After we said our goodbyes to the ladies, I invited Mr. Masterson to join us for coffee.

"Again, please call me Bat. I hope I didn't say something offensive to the ladies."

He'd asked, so, I got straight to the point.

"Yes, you did offend them, Mr. Masterson. The National Police Gazette is not a magazine suitable for women and children. Nor is the subject you wish to discuss."

To my surprise, he chuckled at my response.

"No, it certainly isn't. Dick Fox is a friend of mine, but his magazine *is* disreputable, and I'm quite sure he's already in the process of publishing a sensationalized story of the events up there. Come on, John, I was kidding about wanting to interview you for that particular periodical. It was meant to be a joke. You might be aware of how my own reputation was besmirched in his sordid rag."

"I believe it established your reputation."

"Exactly, and it is largely the reason I am no longer in law enforcement. I'm afraid the same thing may well happen to you."

"...How's that?"

"A man's reputation is almost completely out of his control. I fear you will be presented as a gunslinger, and a mad killer with a badge. Once that image is made public, it will make it quite hard for you to change it."

I nodded. I'd already had far too much experience with the effects of such stories.

"This is bad, John. You really should get out of the public eye, for a while." Tom observed.

"I'm afraid it will not be sufficient to avoid the issue." Bat said.

"What else can I do?"

"I've had a look around North Fork, and talked to some of the people involved on

23

the occasion in question. I also read Tommy Turner's affidavit of the events, which I'm told *you* filed for record in the courthouse. A brilliant move on your part, by the way. My point is this; you need to fight fire with fire. Let me tell the world the way it really happened. I have some notoriety, I really can get the story published in reputable newspapers, and it will be circulated all over the world. When the Police Gazette comes out with their story, it will immediately be seen as an obvious distortion of the facts."

I shook my head.

"Bat, the facts have already been published in newspapers all over the country. The truth is out there."

"Is it? That's why I'm here. The story *has* been told, but not by you. It seems you've refused to comment, and you're avoiding the press. I just want to give you the chance to tell the story, in your own words."

I considered my response.

"Listen, Bat, I appreciate your interest in this, but I made a statement at the time. Further, I've had bad experiences with the press, no offense to you. I don't think me talking about it in print will improve the situation any.

"I understand how you feel, John. What I have in mind is a question and answer interview. You won't have to tell a story, just answer some questions, as I said, in your own words. I won't submit anything for publication you don't approve yourself. What do you say?"

"I'll think about it..."

"Fair enough, I'll ask you again before I leave on Monday. The thing is this; you need to strike while the iron is still hot."

"Yeah, that's the problem. At this moment, it's far too hot. I'm pretty much branded"

3.

On Monday morning, I arrived at the courthouse when the doors opened to have a look at the affidavit I'd tricked Tommy Turner into signing.

"Good morning, Sheriff. What can we do for you today?" Mr. Harold, the County Clerk asked.

"Do you remember the affidavit I had filed for record, a few weeks..."

"...Of course, everybody and their dog have been in here to see it," he interrupted. "In fact, on Friday, Bat Masterson himself was in here and asked to read it."

"No kidding, Bat Masterson?"

"Oh, yes sir. He walked in as bold as brass. A fine looking gentleman, I must say. He didn't look like a..." he trailed off.

27

"Like a what, Mr. Harold?"

"Uhh, a former law man was what I meant."

"May I see the affidavit, please?"

"Certainly, it's filed in Book "H", right over there on the table. I expect it's already open to page one hundred and eleven. I leave it out, so people can get right to it."

"That's very…convenient."

"Yes sir, making public records available to the public. That's just part of my job."

He had indeed left the book open to the correct page.

I read the affidavit.

It was written in the somewhat sloppy, but still quite legible, handwriting of the so called "Sheriff" of North Fork. He provided an abbreviated version of the events which culminated in eight men being killed and several others wounded. It listed those killed by name and stated that six of those men had been wanted outlaws with reward money available to whoever could capture or kill them.

I knew my former deputy Bob Logan had collected all the reward money. I also knew he had plans to use half of the money to build a church in North Fork.

Most importantly, the affidavit indicated I'd been the lone lawman on the scene, entering the Gold Dust Hotel and Casino to affect the arrest of Henry and Harvey Thondyke, on charges related to a bank robbery. I walked into the saloon at the exact moment the celebrated gunman, Wes Spradlin, had engaged his half-brother Andrew "Point Blank" Peterson in a gun fight. Both of those men had been killed in the exchange. The sudden drawing and firing of guns prompted the outlaws to try shooting their way out. I'd been assisted in my attempt to arrest the Thorndyke brothers by Bob Logan, a bounty hunter who had, until recently, been my deputy.

The affidavit was signed by Tommy, me, and two other witnesses.

It was the affidavit I had filed of record, but it wasn't entirely accurate. Wes Spradlin had not been killed in the shooting. I concocted the story to help him get a new start in life.

That was something Bat Masterson didn't need to know, and I intended to make sure he never found out about it.

Since I was already at the courthouse, I decided to check the deed records. I'd been planning to see if I could locate anything that might help me find out where Jacob and Sarah had come from.

I went to the County Tax Assessor first and examined various maps to determine who paid the taxes and therefor probably owned the property around Yellow Butte.

I learned there was a section and a half, nine hundred and sixty acres, along both sides of Buttercup Creek right at the base of Yellow Butte, belonging to a man named Murphy. His taxes were current and paid.

I went back to the County Clerk's office and looked up the deed granting the land to Murphy. It had been conveyed to Sean Murphy twelve years previously, by a man named R.W. Kennemer. It was still owned by Murphy.

I couldn't be sure I had the right tract of land, or that Murphy was the father of Jacob and Sarah, but it was a start.

I had one more thing to look for.

I searched through the brand book and found where Murphy had recorded his brand. It was a rocking M.

Checking my watch I discovered it was nearing ten thirty. I'd promised Bat Masterson I would meet him at the Front Range Hotel and give him my answer before he got on the 12:10 for Denver.

I was aware Bat Masterson was considered to be a friend of the great con artist, Soapy Smith. Smith had been involved in organized crime and crooked politics in Creede and now in Denver. It was rumored Masterson had supported his efforts. It was certain they frequented the same boom towns at the same time.

I checked with the hotel clerk who gave me Bat's room number.

When I knocked on the door, Bat opened it. He was in his shirtsleeves and waistcoat. I wasn't surprised to see he was wearing a handgun in a shoulder holster, similar to mine.

He grinned when he saw me.

"Well, I sure hope this is good news, John. I'm in the process of packing my valise for the trip to Denver."

"It appears you won't be able to make the train."

"And why is that?"

"I expect I'll have to arrest you for carrying a handgun inside the city limits."

He looked startled.

"You're joking...right?"

I shrugged. Then I waved my hand to let him know I wasn't serious.

"OK, here's the deal. I'll agree to the interview, under the terms we discussed. I will not stand for any fun and games. I know you're a great friend of Soapy Smith, but I will not be scammed or conned in any way. Do you understand me?"

He stiffened up a bit.

"My association with Mr. Smith has nothing to do with this. Soapy has considerable influence in Denver and it doesn't work in a man's favor to be on his bad side. He tends to cause problems for people who cross him. As a sporting man, and the way I earn my living these days, I have to stay on his good side, if you know what I mean. Further, I am neither a con man nor a bunko artist. I have offered to interview you in good faith. Sure, I intend to sell the story to whoever will buy it, but I am not taking advantage of you in any way."

He appeared to be sincere. But good con men always do.

Still, I couldn't help liking him, even though I didn't entirely trust him.

"Alright then, I know I delayed you here over the weekend, and I feel kind of bad about it, so I'm inviting you to have lunch at my house, and stay the night with us. Tomorrow, you can catch the 12:10 to Denver.

"Outstanding! That's capital, simply capital. I accept your invitation, as it happens I'm about out of money. Can we sit down and do the interview this afternoon?"

"I think it would be best."

"Well then, give me a few minutes to gather my things…"

DAN ARNOLD

4.

Our house was on the very outskirts of town, on the west side. It was down right beside Bear Creek, the stream for which the city was named.

The house, a huge, two-story whitewashed wooden structure with a wraparound porch, sat on about thirty five acres of land. From our back porch we had a grand view of the mountains.

Before we were married Lora had run a boarding house there, and we continued to take in boarders after we were wed. That all ended when I was shot by one of our guests.

Although we were no longer accepting boarders, Lora decided to continue serving lunch and dinner on the premises. This kept Consuela employed, and made use of the space, without endangering the family. I found it amusing (and rather convenient) I was now living in what was arguably one of the best restaurants in Bear Creek.

It was a mixed blessing.

I had both the opportunity and the responsibility to greet and interact with the visitors. I was aware I might've become an attraction for some folks, kind of like a trained monkey, a caged bear or some such oddity.

I'd smoothed things over with Lora, and she agreed to allow Bat Masterson to stay with us until the next day. It turned out he was something of an attraction himself.

At lunch, we discovered Bat was an accomplished raconteur. He held our guests spellbound as he told them stories about his time in the west.

RIDING FOR THE BRAND

We learned, as one of the buffalo hunters in the second battle of Adobe Walls, he helped hold off a combined force of Comanche and Kiowa for three days.

That was interesting to me, because my friend, Yellow Horse, was on the other side in that fight.

Bat went on with stories about living in various boom towns. He never mentioned his days as a deputy to Wyatt Earp in Dodge City.

"Yessiree, now, Creede is *the* place to be. She's going to be a great city. Folks, I'm telling you, money flows like water there and so does the whiskey.

I arrived in that delightful locale right at the start of the boom. There were dozens of new minors arriving every day.

King silver lined our pockets, until the fire swept through town. Most of the buildings were just tents and slap together shanties. I had a fine gambling hall, but the fire wiped us out. My place was burned to the ground and there was nothing left, not so much as a single unbroken glass. Why, even the paper money inside my safe was all burned up. That fire nearly destroyed the whole town, but Creede can't be kept down. No sir! She'll come back bigger and better than ever." He paused for effect.

"Isn't that the way it goes, folks? One day I was a well-established, wealthy, and prosperous business man. The next day we were all vagrants, and poor as church mice.

One day, boom, the next day, bust. The town is still booming, but we're busted. My wife and I are forced to make a new start in Denver," he concluded.

"What brings you to Bear Creek, Mr. Masterson?" Someone asked.

"Well, I had planned to open a gentleman's sporting club up in North Fork. I intended to sponsor prize fights and other similar propositions, but now I find myself without sufficient funds to do so. I decided to have a look around and see if the climate was healthy enough to risk securing a loan for the purpose.

I'm given to understand the mines are not paying out as well as they were. And recent events," he glanced at me, "have changed the climate up there. So, I'm exploring new opportunities."

"Have you considered Bear Creek? We have a fair grounds and rodeo arena. We even have horse racing. I would think this would be an ideal location for a prize fighting venue. Maybe you and the Missus should plan to move up here, from Denver?"

"That is a possibility. I'm considering my options. Today, I'm just spending some time visiting with my friend John, here."

Lora narrowed her eyes and glanced my way.

It was pretty clear she did not like our house guest.

***

When the lunch crowd eventually cleared out, I sat down with Bat to do the interview.

"I understand you were in Dodge City with Wyatt Earp and Doc Holiday. Is that correct?" I asked, seeking some common ground.

"Yep, me and my brothers and Wyatt and his brothers, were all the law that was needed in Dodge. It's where I first met Doc."

"I met Doc Holliday in Dallas, years ago. He filled a tooth for me. He got into a

42

shooting scrape there and had to leave town in a hurry. I never saw him again after that." I said.

"Well, I did. I saw him again in Tombstone, Arizona. I was going to work for Wyatt, but there was an incident in Dodge City which required my attention, so I went back to Kansas. I never saw Doc again. He died right here in Colorado, just a few years ago."

"I know. I heard he died in bed."

"Yep, he finally wasted away. I always figured he would go out in a blaze of glory. He was a man who should've died with his boots on, but the consumption finally got him. It sure took a lot longer than anyone thought it would."

We sat in silence for a moment.

"Are you ready to tell me about what happened up at North Fork?" He asked.

I nodded.

"Sure, but the story didn't start there. Let me tell you a somewhat longer tale."

Bat licked the end of his pencil, and nodded expectantly.

***

When we were done with the whole story, he started asking questions to clear up the details.

"Are you sure Martin Pogue was one of the men killed?"

"Yes, I am."

"Well, I'm glad to hear it. He was a bad outlaw. If any man deserved to die in a pool of his own blood, it was Martin Pogue."

"We all do." I observed.

"Pardon me?"

"I said we all deserve to die horribly."

"I don't see it that way."

"Bat, my point is we're all sinners. We want to look at other people and see their sin, but we don't want to recognize our own."

"Speak for yourself, sir!"

I nodded. "I am speaking for myself. But, be honest, you must agree your choices have often included certain attitudes and activities which are not above reproach."

"Reproach from whom? I don't believe society has the right to determine what is, or is not, acceptable behavior for me, or anyone else."

"I wasn't speaking about society, but it strikes me as an odd position for a lawman to take."

"When I was a lawman, I enforced the law because without it, in those places, there would've been complete anarchy. I didn't have any sense it was important to have a bunch of laws to regulate people's individual morality."

"Now, Bat, I'm sure you would agree there are some folks who just don't have much sense or self-control. People lie, cheat and steal. It just comes naturally. Unless we recognize and confess our sin, God will not forgive or change us. It's an important part of being a Christian."

"Perhaps, but I am not one of them. I believe self-preservation is the only true morality. In this life you have to take advantage of every opportunity to get ahead. No one is going to give you anything. You have to find a way to get it for yourself."

"So, you don't worry much about sin?"

"What is sin? If a person wants to gamble, I see no harm in it. The same could be said for drinking and carousing. I imagine most folks would call those things sin, but a little of that now and then is harmless enough. It's how I make my living. There's always some sucker who's just asking to be taken advantage of."

"Spoken like a true sporting man, Bat."

"Oh yes, I am that, John," He grinned.

Bat's attitude worried me. I was concerned he'd become a complete reprobate.

I walked over to a side table and took a deck of cards out of a drawer.

"Perhaps you would be interested in a little game of cards." I said, shuffling the deck.

"What do you have in mind?"

I fanned the cards, and selected three. I dealt them face up on the table. One of them was the Queen of Hearts. I turned the cards over, face down.

"…Three card Monte? You've got to be kidding me." He exclaimed.

I quickly slid the three cards around, with a flourish.

"Let's call this game 'Follow the Queen'. You just have to guess which card is the Queen of Hearts. Would you care to bet on it?"

"I know what it's called. I also know I can't win. You've used some sort of sleight of hand to palm the Queen." Bat said. "Where did you learn to do that? You're as good as anyone I've ever seen."

"Perhaps you would rather play the Shell game?"

"Of course not, what do you take me for?"

"I take you for a sporting man, Bat."

"Now see here. If you're suggesting I'm a cheat or scam artist...As I said, you are mistaken sir."

"No, Bat, I'm not suggesting you're a scam artist. I'm telling you I used to be one.

I learned to play these 'games' when I was still just a kid. I grew up in a traveling carnival. I got to be pretty good at sleight of hand tricks.

We Romani would sometimes take advantage of the ignorant and the 'sucker' you referred to earlier. We did little harm and then we moved on. But I felt remorse for the deception.

I know people who are very good as short change artists and a host of other two bit tricks. You know, Bat, the short cons like these, they're all as crooked as a dog's hind leg. You might think they're harmless. But wrong is wrong.

49

There are also people who are good at the long cons. Those cons that take hours, days, or even weeks to put in place, and tend to pay off with big rewards of money stolen from people you call "suckers."

"I told you...I don't do that."

"I heard you. I'm not saying *you* do. However I have to consider the company you keep. My point is; I'm not a sucker. Don't ever mistake me for one. Do we understand each other?"

"Why, John, you've wounded me. I've given you my assurance I will not attempt to take advantage of you, in any way."

"I'm taking you at your word for it, Bat"

"It would not appear you do."

"You correctly told me a man's reputation is largely out of his control. I know you have a long standing association with Soapy Smith. Need I say more?"

Bat hung his head.

"No, I hear what you're saying. The man sticks to me like a bad smell. He has a lot of power in Denver, and he practically ran Creede."

"That bad smell you speak of is the smell of corruption. It's what sin always leads to. No man should ever have to try to convince other people he's not a crook, especially not a man like you. I'd get shut of Soapy, if I were you."

"I intend to." He said, looking me in the eye.

Sin is real and always destructive of whoever embraces it. Sin isn't so much a particular act, as it is a matter of the heart, a sickness of soul. The wages of sin is death.

There is a spiritual death as well as a physical one.

It's not my place to judge another man's heart or know his ultimate destiny. Bat had attempted to befriend me, so I put out my hand.

"That's good enough for me."

We shook on it.

5.

The next morning, I was out of the house early and arrived in my office in the courthouse only to find it already occupied.

"Morning, John." Buckskin Charlie Owens said, as though we met like this every day.

Buckskin Charlie Owens had recently been an exhibition shooter in a traveling Wild West show. He could do amazing things with a handgun, or pretty much any type of long gun. He'd been billed as "Buckskin Charlie Owens, the world's finest marksman and fast draw artist." These days, he'd cut his hair, and he seldom wore the double holsters, or the fancy fringed buckskin coat, which had been part of his stage persona. He still had a big bushy walrus mustache. He'd been well on

53

his way to becoming a famous entertainer, but Charlie had gotten sick of show business. Most folks still thought of him as "Buckskin" Charlie.

Before the Wild West show, he'd been a little known and underappreciated law man. I was thrilled when he accepted my job invitation. I'd recently promoted him to Chief Deputy.

This morning, he was sitting at my desk in my "official" office on the first floor of the courthouse. We had another office downstairs in the basement, near the jail. That was his usual post, but with me out these last couple of weeks, he'd taken custody of my office.

"I suppose you want your desk back…"He said, as he started to stand.

"No, Charlie. You stay right there."

He raised his eyebrows.

"I just came in to tell you I'm going to be gone for a little while longer."

"Oh, alright, I understand. I sure am looking forward to you coming back though. I hate having to be the man in this office. Now I understand a little about how President Cleveland must feel."

I grinned.

"Kinda makes you appreciate the bad guys, huh?"

"Shoot yes! I'd rather spend my time with the men locked up downstairs than have to deal with the people who walk into this office. I swear; the criminals are more honest and less likely to stab you in the back."

"I know what you mean. Listen, I'm going to attend the meeting of the Board of Commissioners tonight, so you won't have to be there. I've got some things to talk over with them."

He nodded.

"Appreciate it, but I'll be there anyway, if you don't mind."

"I don't mind at all, Charlie. I just don't want you to feel like you have to."

He nodded once and changed the subject.

"How are you feeling, John, you healing up alright?"

"Good, Charlie, I'm doing fine. I just need some time to work out some personal stuff."

"You bet. Don't worry; we've got the duties of the Sheriff's department pretty much under control."

"Have you heard anything from Ed?"

I'd left orders to send my deputy, Ed Burnside, up to North Fork. I'd sent him up there after the shooting trouble in the town. He was supposed to stay up there for two weeks, or until the worst of the riff raff had pulled out. It all started, when the Governor instructed me to put an end to the open corruption, prostitution, and gambling up at North Fork. I'd given the town notice they had one month to get it done. Two weeks into the month, I found myself shooting it out with some bad outlaws.

"He came in late last night. I haven't seen him yet this morning." Charlie said.

"Seen who?" Ed asked, from the open doorway.

"Hah, just the man I was looking for." I said.

We shook hands.

"Sheriff, I heard you'd been shot. You look a little the worse for wear, are you OK?"

"I'm fine, and you're a sight for sore eyes. I was afraid I was gonna have to ride up there to check on you. Has there been any trouble?"

"No sir. The local 'sheriff', Tommy Turner, hasn't been much help, but he never tried to interfere with me. I've had to say and do some things to get the point across, but I haven't had to deal with any really strong resistance. I'll bet fifty people have pulled out of town, in the last couple of weeks."

"I'm glad to hear it. I knew I could count on you."

"Yes sir, but I think I'll need to go back up there. Least ways, someone will have to. I don't mean to say Tommy Turner can't be trusted..."

"...But Tommy Turner can't be trusted." Charlie and I chimed in.

We all shrugged, simultaneously.

"That's one of the things I need to address with the Board of Commissioners tonight." I observed. "If you're willing to go back up there, I can't think of anyone better than you."

"Yes sir, but I need some things…"

"Whatever you need to do your job, I'll see you get it."

"Yes sir, only do you think maybe I could get my pay?"

I looked at Charlie.

"I've got your pay right here," he said, opening one of my desk drawers. "I wasn't sure how I was supposed to get it to you, Ed."

***

When I left the courthouse I walked over to the livery stable. I spent some time grooming Dusty. I hadn't seen him much since I'd been shot.

I saw Alexander Granville Dorchester III, the proprietor of the livery stable, approaching.

"Hey, Al," I said, my usual greeting.

I needed to discuss the matter of Dusty's board. The county was paying to have Dusty boarded here at the livery stable. If I took him home with me, Al could lose some income.

There was considerable convenience to having him at the livery stable. Al took good care of him, sparing me having to feed him at least twice a day, and keeping his feet properly shod.

Then again, we had good pasture down by the creek and our barn had stalls. Our two carriage horses were quite content there.

"Al, I'm thinking about moving Dusty down to my place. What do you think about that?"

Al nodded thoughtfully.

"Sure would beat having to hike up the hill into town every day, especially when the snow falls. You can ride him up here, and ride back down in the evening. I know he would enjoy having some room to roam around and roll in that good grass you have down there. It isn't natural for a horse to have to be penned up all the time." He said.

"Maybe the county would still pay his board bill, if I had him boarded here during the day." I mused.

"Well, you do what you think is best. You know I'm pretty fond of him myself."

"I'm gonna give it a try. Jake wants to ride him some."

"How are those kids doing? I kind of miss having them around here," he said.

"Do you, really?"

"No, not really, it's not safe here for children, and they worried me some."

"It was kind of you to let them hide here, not chasing them off."

"Yeah, well…"

"Tonight, at the meeting of the Board of Commissioners, I'm going to address the issue about all the orphans in town."

"Good. I'll come to the meeting myself."

"You might want to speak to some other folks about the meeting, too. It would be good if some of the more prominent town folk were there."

He squinted at me. "Say now, it's a good idea and I'm gonna do exactly that."

6.

Back at the house, Bat and I had an early lunch and then walked back into town together so he could catch the 12:10 to Denver.

When we got to the top of the hill near the courthouse, we stopped for a moment. Bat was red faced and sweating. By the way he bent over; I could tell he had a stitch in his side. He looked up at me.

"I can see you're not fully recovered, John. You look a bit peaked. Are you feeling alright?" He stayed bent over, panting a little.

I chuckled. "You're the second person to say that to me, today. All this walking back and forth is the most exercise I've had in over two weeks. I'm fine though. I just need to build up my strength."

Bat nodded. "You'll be back in fighting form in no time. I'm a bit winded from the hike myself."

"It's the altitude, not the grade or the distance,"

"It's all that, and more," he replied, patting his ample belly.

We both chuckled at the comment.

At the depot, we stood there talking as the train came whistling down the tracks and chugged to a steamy halt at the platform.

We waited for the arriving passengers to get off, one of whom caught Bat's attention.

"I say, Theodore, is that you?"

"Why, Bat Masterson, bully to see you!" The man responded. He struck a pugilist's pose, fists extended, grinning a toothy grin. Bat matched his pose for a moment, the two men looking remarkably alike.

"Hah! What are you doing in Bear Creek, Theodore?"

"Just stretching my legs, I'm on my way to Denver, and then back to the city. How about you? Are you still in the fight game?"

Bat waggled his hand, indicating ambiguity.

"Theodore, let me introduce you to my friend John Everett Sage. John, this is Theodore Roosevelt. You two have something in common."

"How do you do Mr. Roosevelt," I said, shaking his hand.

"Are you *the* Sheriff Sage, the celebrated shootist? I wonder what we might have in common." The man said, looking me in the eye.

"You're both in law enforcement, Theodore. That's what you have common. John, Theodore is the Police Commissioner for the city of New York."

"Well, that's impressive. You're a long way from home, Mr. Roosevelt."

"I have some land in North Dakota, Wyoming and Montana. I had a cattle operation, but the winter of '87 did me in, wiped out my entire herd. I'm still in love with the west. Beautiful country, I come out here whenever I can."

"Theodore is something of a reformer, John. He's cleaning up the police force in New York City."

"I imagine it will take some doing." I observed.

"I've heard you know how to deal with corruption yourself, Sheriff Sage. Bully for you!"

"You can't believe everything you read in the papers."

Nodding his understanding, Theodore looked thoughtful for a moment.

"I believe we may have another friend in common, besides old Bat here."

"Who might that be?"

"Do you know John Browning?"

I grinned.

"Yes, I surely do."

"Board! All aboooard!" The conductor called.

"That's us, Theodore." Bat said. "John, thanks for your hospitality and consideration. Don't worry. I'll see your story gets properly published."

"Good bye, Bat. Mr. Roosevelt, it was a pleasure to meet you." I said, shaking hands all around.

The two men turned and boarded the train, each stepping aside for the other, Theodore finally boarding before Bat. The two looking so alike, they could've been brothers.

As the train pulled away from the station I thought about what a strange man Bat Masterson was. Imagine him knowing the Police Commissioner for the city of New York! Bat was something of a rascal and Theodore was a hard-nosed reformer, but clearly, they were friends.

***

I found Tom in his office at the police station.

"Good afternoon, Chief. What's new with you?"

"Well, howdy, Sheriff Sage. I'm just going over the reports. I don't know what to do with these sagebrush orphans. We've got a crime wave going on."

I wondered if Tom had made the sagebrush orphan reference because he knew it was how I got my name.

I'd been one of those sagebrush orphans. They called me a sagebrush kid, eventually just "that sage kid", and the name had stuck.

Life can be especially harsh and unforgiving, west of the Mississippi. Many of these orphaned kids were the unwanted children of prostitutes, while others were children whose parents had been lost to the sudden calamities common throughout the west.

"They're stealing just about anything that's not nailed down. My officers have caught several of them, but I can't lock em up in my jail *or* yours. They're just kids. The crimes have been mostly petty thefts so far, but it's just a matter of time till something worse happens." He said.

"I'm going to address the issue with the county Board of Commissioners tonight. I got a letter from Mrs. Poole, or I should say Mrs. Bradley, the preacher's wife. She detailed specific terms for the administration of her gift, and included the deed to the property up at North Fork. We can have a fully functional orphanage within a matter of weeks, maybe even sooner, once we get the commissioners to sign off on the deal."

Tom smiled. "You wouldn't mind if I came to the meeting and addressed the commissioners myself, would you?"

"I thought you'd never ask."

"When are the uhhh, 'Bradley's' coming back?"

I knew Tom was referring to the Reverend Jeff Bradley and his new bride, Emma Bradley, our friends who were formerly known by other, more notorious, names.

"It probably won't be long. Once people stop coming to see the place where the famed gunfighter, Wes Spradlin, was killed, and others forget Mrs. Bradley was once the legendary Mrs. Poole who ran some rather successful bordellos…"

"Yeah, it wouldn't do to have Wes Spradlin suddenly resurrected in our midst, would it?" Tom speculated.

"No. But, Ed tells me about fifty of the outlaws, tramps and losers have pulled out of North Fork. That's most or all of the people who might've known either Wes or Emma in their previous lives. I'm confident they'll be able to start a new life in North Fork."

"It's a better chance than most folks get. It'll be a new life for both them and the town."

"God willing, things are turning around up there. The deal with the logging company is pretty much done. There'll be a new sawmill and new families moving into North Fork, before the snow flies."

"They'll have a new church and a new preacher as well." Tom added. "I hear they've already started construction."

"And the county orphanage," I pointed out

"I expect the Governor is pleased, John. You've accomplished more than he asked you to do."

I shrugged.

"I haven't heard from him and I don't expect I will. He's probably distancing himself as far from me as he can, at least until the ruckus dies down. He doesn't want people to think he sent a killer up there to clean up the town with gunfire."

"Politics, John. Both of your careers start and end with politics. He's an elected official, just like you are."

"So you keep reminding me."

DAN ARNOLD

7.

Politics has never interested me, but as Tom is fond of reminding me, I'm an elected official. It's an aspect of the Sheriff's job I do not enjoy.

Part of the responsibility involves going to the monthly County Board of Commissioner's meetings. Because I'm a county employee, I'm answerable to the Board of Commissioners. It's through them all business matters of the Sheriff's department are funded and approved.

To say I got a mixed reception at the meeting would be an understatement.

It was clear the commissioners had already been talking to each other and had chosen sides. About half of them were happy to see me and greeted me warmly, enquiring about my recovery. The other half wouldn't even make eye contact with me and gave me the brush off as quickly as they could.

It didn't help that the local newspaper, *The Bear Creek Banner*, openly opposed me at every turn. It really irked me, because they'd found in me an abundance of colorful stories (mostly fabricated) which improved both their circulation and revenue from advertising.

It was evident the commissioners were surprised at the attendance of this seemingly routine board meeting.

The seven of them were seated behind a couple of tables pushed together in front of the Judge's bench in the courthouse. They were facing the rows of seats in the gallery, now fully occupied by the citizens in attendance. There were even people leaning against the walls.

Not expecting much of a turn-out, the commissioners had only printed about fifteen copies of the agenda, not nearly enough for all the people in attendance.

There was a continuous murmur of voices as the citizens of the county discussed the meeting. The atmosphere was...expectant.

The chairman struck his gavel to bring the meeting to order. They started by reading the minutes of the previous month's meeting and voted to accept them as read. They moved on to old business generated by the previous meeting.

As usual, there was a long discussion about manure disposal and the need to limit the horse traffic in town. Maybe the county should build a wagon yard just outside town, where people could park their rigs and manure pickup would be much easier.

Eventually someone moved the matter be tabled because it was more of a city issue than a county issue, and no one from the city had officially requested it. It was quickly seconded and the vote was called. The vote to table the matter was, as usual, unanimous.

When the old business had all been addressed, it was time to move on to the matters listed on the agenda for this meeting. Most of it was routine and related to collection and distribution of revenues, which eventually brought them to the issues involving the County Sheriff's office.

"Sheriff Sage, we're glad to see you're feeling well enough to represent your department in this meeting. We have a number of concerns to address..." The chairman started. "First, let me say we find your recent conduct entirely..."

"Excuse me, Mr. Chairman. My conduct is not listed on the agenda for this meeting. There are, however, other issues which *are* on the agenda. As a point of order, don't you think we should address those items on the printed agenda? I believe public discussion of my conduct might have to wait until we get to new business."

The resulting murmur from the crowd was not wasted on the chairman.

"Hmmm. Yes, of course. I see here you have requested additional deputies, once again. I don't see any need for …"

"Excuse me, Mr. Chairman. I believe this is the time when I'm supposed to explain my request and outline the benefits to the county. Are you calling for a vote without discussion?"

"Well, no but…"

"My department now has one less deputy since the last meeting of this board. Additionally, the county is providing a law enforcement presence up at North Fork. As you may be aware, at the request of the Governor, all open gambling and prostitution has been shut down in North Fork…"

"We all know what you've done, and how you did it. You're nothing but a two bit gunman…" The chairman started.

The sound of the angry protests from the crowd drowned out his next words. Two of the committee members rose to their feet and began shouting at the chairman, who began pounding his gavel in earnest. When order was restored, he tried again.

"I apologize for my previous remark, Sheriff Sage. The fact I personally find your behavior to be reprehensible should not affect the course of this meeting. Please conclude your remarks so we can vote on the matter."

"My point is this, Mr. Chairman. The sheriff's department is actively engaged in law enforcement throughout the county, enforcing ordinances, collecting fines, seizing property, managing the jail, transporting prisoners and providing security at trials. We just don't have enough men to do it all as well as it should be done.

As you know, there was a recent jailbreak. It could've been avoided if I had more deputies. The county continues to grow in population and tax revenue continues to increase, but I now have fewer deputies than I had last month."

The crowd began to murmur again. I saw Jerry Starnes, the publisher, reporter, printer and owner of the *Bear Creek Banner,* writing furiously with his pencil.

I spoke up a little louder.

"I need to keep a deputy up at North Fork, and another out at Waller. It takes hours to get to either of those locations and we only go there in response to a problem. The people of those communities pay taxes just like the citizens of Bear Creek. They have a right to feel their law enforcement needs are being met as well. I need at least three more deputies in order to effectively provide for the law enforcement needs of the people of this county."

The crowd continued to murmur in agreement.

The chairman banged his gavel again.

"Does that conclude your remarks, Sheriff Sage?"

"On this part of the agenda, yes sir."

"Fine, we'll vote on it then."

"Hang on, Jed. The other members of the committee are entitled to discuss the matter before it comes up for a vote." One of the commissioners pointed out.

"Very well, is there any discussion?"

"I'd like to say something," Tom said, as he stood up from his seat in the crowd.

"I'm sorry, Chief Smith, but we can't include members of the public in this discussion. It is a matter of order. You'll have to save any comments until we move on to new business."

"Well now, Jed, it seems to me the Chief of Police isn't just an ordinary member of the public. Because he's actively involved in law enforcement too, I'll let him make his comment in my place." One of the other commissioners offered.

"Uhh, I don't know if you can do that..."

"…Won't take me but a minute." Tom said.

"Well, please be brief."

"Sheriff Sage is the best lawman I've ever met. He's been a very good friend to my department. I have prisoners in his jail almost every day. When the bank was robbed, he was the one who tracked the robbers and it was his hard work that eventually nearly got him killed, just a couple of weeks ago."

The crowd buzzed in agreement.

"Chief Smith, is there some point to this story?" The chairman asked.

"Yes sir, the point is as the Chief of Police for the city of Bear Creek, I think the Sheriff should get whatever he asks for." Tom said.

The crowd roared in agreement.

The chairman banged his gavel and waited for the crowd to settle down.

"Is there any further discussion?" He asked.

When there was no response from the other commissioners, the chairman called for a vote. The vote was five to two in favor of my getting three new deputies. I'd been hoping there was a slim chance I might get even one!

We had some other minor issues to discuss and the only vote taken was to accept my report as given.

"As this concludes the agenda items, I'll ask if there is any new business to be brought before the board of commissioners," the Chairman said, with eager anticipation.

Before he had the chance to begin a discussion of my performance, I spoke up.

"Yes, there is."

The chairman scowled.

"Sheriff, why didn't you mention this before and have it added to the agenda."

"I just received a letter today which prompts me to bring the matter to your attention."

"And what is this matter?"

"It's about the orphans. We're all aware in the last few weeks; there've been a large number of incidents of petty theft which appear to have been the work of unattended children. These children don't have anyone to take care of them and they're learning to take care of themselves, by any means necessary. The problem is nearly unmanageable now, and it will only get worse unless we do something about it."

"As you said, we're all aware of the problem, Sheriff Sage. We don't know who these children are or where they came from. I suppose we could round them up and ship them off to some sort of state run work facility. What would that cost?" The chairman asked.

There was an angry murmur from the crowd.

"Such action would be rather cruel, and it wouldn't solve the problem. May I share the contents of the letter I mentioned?"

"Proceed." The chairman said, with some reluctance.

"This letter details the terms of the gift to the county of about twenty five acres of land and a large house in excellent condition. I'll skip the personal parts and just read the pertinent details.

"The land and the house are a gift to Alta Vista County, subject to the following provisions; The land and house are to be used by the county for one purpose and one purpose only, that being the establishment

and maintenance of an orphanage to house and care for any and all orphaned children found within the boundaries of Alta Vista County. The house and land may not be sold by the county or used for any purpose other than the establishment and maintenance of the Alta Vista County orphanage".

The crowd interrupted me with a round of applause and cheering. When the hubbub died down, I resumed my appeal.

"The deed to the property is included with the letter, Mr. Chairman. There is also a monetary gift, which is to be used to provision the house with such furnishings and facilities as may be needed to house and feed the orphaned children."

There was more applause from the crowd.

"There is however one additional proviso the county must accept, or the gift will not be made." I said, not at all happy at having to mention it.

"And that is?" asked the chairman.

I read the statement as written in the letter.

"This gift is contingent on each and every one of these provisions being fully met; failure to meet any one of these provisions will negate the deed and cause forfeiture of the gift. The final provision herein is that the property and the orphanage once established on it, is from henceforth and in perpetuity to be called ...The John Everett Sage Children's Home of Alta Vista County."

DAN ARNOLD

8.

When the racket finally died down, there was considerable discussion and several members of the public were very clear about how they would vote in future elections if the county failed to adopt the proposal.

It was stated by several people that if any one of the current county commissioners did not vote to accept the gift and get the orphanage started, right away, they needn't be concerned about running for office in the future.

The vote accepting the gift with its full provisions was eventually approved. Then they tried to postpone any discussion of funding for the orphanage for a month, until the next meeting. That met with substantial rancor from the assembled multitudes. There was even some name calling. Finally the commissioners agreed to conduct a special meeting in one week to set the budget for the orphanage, allowing them time to do some research on what might be reasonable expenses.

I knew Emma had put that last provision in as a way to thumb her nose at the stuffed shirts who ran the county. She hadn't consulted me and it came as a shock when I read it.

I was generally pleased with the way the commissioners meeting had gone, but I knew my enemies would be even more galvanized because of it. That was confirmed in my view when I read *the Bear Creek Banner* the next day.

Shifty Sheriff Shafts the County

RIDING FOR THE BRAND

The Alta Vista County Board of Commissioners were stunned last night to learn that our gunslinger Sheriff, John Everett Sage, has used his position to coerce a woman of ill repute into donating a certain property (that had once been a house of iniquity) to the county. Apparently, not only has Sheriff Sage extorted the property from this poor unfortunate woman, but he has browbeaten her into having the property named after him!

This reporter has learned the woman was once a citizen of this county and a resident of Bear Creek. She was forced to flee this area in fear and loathing of our gun happy Sheriff. No doubt she fled in fear for her very life!

Citizens are outraged

This is the same Sheriff Sage, who took it upon himself to go to the town of North

Fork and gun down anyone he thought was operating a business he was not personally profiting from. This reporter has learned that Sheriff Sage put a county employee in residence (at the county's expense) in North Fork to enforce the sheriff's rule. Perhaps now, he will be able to enjoy the additional income from the proceeds of all his shady business in that community!

The State of Colorado is shocked and scandalized

I couldn't bring myself to read any more of the story, which nearly filled the front page.

"You've got to let it go, John." Tom said. "You saw yourself how much support you had at the meeting last night."

"Sure, but that didn't get reported did it? Not only did they distort the story, but they didn't even mention there was going to be an orphanage."

"Well that's the thing that matters. I've instructed my officers to start locating as many of these kids as possible. For now, we're just going to determine how many there are and where they are. Once we get the orphanage staffed. We'll start gathering them up."

"How many do you think there are?"

"There are four or five who are more than ten years old, and we think there are another five or six younger than that. We know at least three or four of them are girls. There could be ten or even a dozen orphaned kids on the street, all together."

"The house could handle almost twice that many, easy. We figured with a little modification it could house as many as twenty four, with a married couple in residence as well. When we first started talking about this, the local churches were going to provide staffing, but now that we know the orphanage is going to be up at North Fork, it won't be feasible." I said.

"True, but I'll bet we can get the churches to either take up special offerings, or agree to help local families adopt one or some of these children. They'll still want to be a part of this and support it somehow."

"You're right, they will. Tom, I know of a woman up at North Fork who would love to cook and clean at the orphanage. I just don't know how to get her hired. If I so much as open my mouth, the newspaper will have her run out of town on a rail.

Tom grinned. "…Right behind you."

"We can get this thing staffed and running before the snow flies up there, but only if I'm not involved. If I have anything further to do with it, I'm afraid the commissioners will find a way to shut it down, indefinitely. We'll need to make arrangements for everything before the meeting next week. The burden for that is going to fall on you."

"I'll handle it. I'll start talking to certain people and get some financial pledges all lined up. If the commissioners try to pull some delaying tactic, we'll fund the start-up privately. That should embarrass the county into action."

"It's a good plan, but don't count on the commissioners being embarrassed into action. If they find out there are plans to fund the start-up without financial support from the county …It would probably make them happy."

"Don't worry, John, I have a few aces up my sleeve."

"Yeah, I'll bet you do at that."

"We'll get it handled."

"There's something else I need to ask of you, Tom."

"OK, what is it."

"I'm planning to leave town for a little while. Just a few days probably, but Lora hates to be alone, and well, I need to know they'll be safe. Will you and Becky stay with her and the kids at night, while I'm gone?"

"I'll have to talk to Becky about it, John. I'll bet she won't mind not having to cook for a few days," he grinned.

"I hate to impose, but there's nobody else I can count on. Besides, Becky is Lora's best friend."

"I know it, and Becky really enjoys playing with those kids."

"You'll have your own child soon. When is Becky due, November, right?"

"Doc says probably the middle of November, only about ten more weeks."

"That *will* be cause for thanksgiving!" I slapped him on the back.

"Where are you planning to go, John?"

"I've wanted to see if I can learn what became of Jake and Sarah's parents. I've been to the courthouse and found the property deed. It has pretty clear calls and landmark references. Jake tells me they lived right below Yellow Butte, so I guess I'll start there. I may be able to locate a relative or someone who has a claim on them."

"John, you're not planning to give them up are you? It seems to me those kids have grown mighty fond of you, and you of them. I've never heard you call Jacob 'Jake' before."

"No. I can't even imagine giving them up, but it would be wrong to keep them from their rightful family. What if they have folks down there who are grieving over their loss?"

He nodded his agreement.

"Well, I'll bet a little change of pace will be good for you. Getting out and seeing some new country, and not having the full weight of the Sheriff's office riding you, is bound to feel good. I wish I could go with you."

"I wish you could too."

"I expect you and Dusty will do just fine. Don't give another thought to what's going on here. Just stretch your legs and clear your head. It'll do you good to have a break from law enforcement."

9.

"John, promise me you'll be careful out there." Lora said.

We were piled up in the bed. The kids were still asleep.

"I guess I'm about the most careful man I know. Besides, I'm just going to be scouting around in search of some kin to Jake and Sarah."

"It seems like any time you ride off, I never know for sure if you will be coming back."

"Baby, I'll always come back to you."

"Well, this time make sure you don't come back all shot up."

"Now, *that* is sound advice."

"It isn't advice, it's an ultimatum." She slapped me playfully on the chest.

"Fair enough, but I'm not going to be hot on the trail of an escaping outlaw or tracking renegades. I'm just out for a pleasant ride in new country. This is personal business, not law enforcement."

"I hope you don't find any of their kin folks, John. I love Sarah and Jake. I can't imagine having to give them up."

I knew how she felt. I couldn't imagine doing it either.

"What about you, John? Could you give them up so easily? She sat up suddenly and looked me in the eye. "I mean it. John, please tell me you love them as much as I do…"

"Yes, I do, baby. I sure do. I don't want to give them up, but it's only right we at least try to get them back with their own family."

"We are their family now, John!"

I nodded, trying to ignore the sudden rush of emotion that was causing my eyes to water. What was wrong with me? I had a lump in my throat and it wasn't like me.

"They love us too, John. I know they do. You know it, don't you?"

I nodded again, still unable to speak.

"You're right though. I knew this day would have to come. We always said we would try to find any family they might have. It's the right thing to do. Now is the time. Putting it off won't change anything. It would just make it that much harder to let go." She conceded.

"There are other things I'd like to know." I mumbled.

"What do you mean?"

"Did their mother get a decent burial? All we know is she'd been sick and when she died, the kids let the milk cow go, and they walked to Bear Creek.

What happened to their father? All we know is he was killed somewhere away from their home.

Why did they walk barefoot all the way to Bear Creek? Those are just some of the questions I would like to have answered."

"Me too," she agreed.

***

At breakfast, the kids were almost chatty.

"Do you think we could ride on Dusty today?" Jake asked me?

"No, not today, Jake. I have to go out of town for a while. Dusty and I will be gone for a few days."

I saw Jacob pale when I told him that.

"I'll probably be back before you start school. We'll have plenty of time to play and ride Dusty then." I promised.

Jacob didn't answer. I could see he was disappointed, but he was frightened as well. After all, his father had ridden off one day and never come back, not alive anyway. Then, just when they were beginning to feel safe with us, there'd been the shooting in our home. I suspected Jake was afraid of things he couldn't even begin to speak of.

"I'm not going away on Sheriff's business. I'm just trying to find somebody who lives in another part of the country. Have you ever heard the name Murphy?"

"...Murphy? That was my pa's name. Everybody called him Mr. Murphy."

"What did they call your mother?" Lora asked gently.

"Uhh, they called her Mrs. Murphy, mostly, I guess."

I could see our questions had brought back some sad memories for Jacob.

"Are there any more people named Murphy around here that you know of?"

"Naw, we was the onlyest ones."

"I'm riding out to see if I can find anybody who may be kin to you and Sarah." I said.

"Well, how will you find um?" He asked.

"I might not. There may not be anybody to find. I may just end up riding around for a while, and then I'll come home."

"That's not so bad..." Jacob said.

"Naw, probably just a waste of time, but I need to do it while the weather is still good."

Mentioning the change in weather prompted a different concern.

"I don't see why I have to go to some stinkin' old school." Jake observed.

"That's because education is very important. Don't you want to learn how to read and write?" Lora asked him.

"Nope."

"Wouldn't you like to be able to add and subtract and learn your numbers?"

"Nope."

"Well then, how about meeting some other children and making new friends?"

"Nope."

"Why don't you want to go to school, Jake?" I asked him.

He looked at me with his hands on his hips and then pointed a finger at me.

"You don't go to no stinkin' school."

Now I understood. He wanted to be like me. I was flattered and a little bit stunned.

"Jake, buddy, I already went to school. I know how to read and write, I can do figures, and I've learned all kinds of useful things. If you don't go to school, you won't ever learn any of the things I know how to do.

He thought about it for a moment.

"You could teach me."

"I could, but I have a job of work to do. I'm the Sheriff of the county and folks expect me to do the Sheriff's job. You have to go to school. That's your job. You're going, and that's all there is to it."

"OK, I'll go, but I won't like it."

I chuckled at that.

"I don't think you should make up your mind until you've tried it."

Lora smiled at me with a twinkle in her eye.

108

"I'll tell you what, Jake, how about you and I hike up into town, and then we can ride Dusty back down here to the house together?" I suggested.

"OK, let's go! Come on, what're you waitin' for?" He began tugging on my hand.

***

At the livery stable, after we got Dusty all groomed and saddled, we said goodbye to Al and rode down to the house. Jake sat behind the cantle and held on to me. We trotted occasionally and I could feel Jake trying not to bounce off from behind me. Dusty has a pretty nice and smooth trot, but Jacob wasn't used to riding yet. At the house, we left Dusty standing at the hitching rail while we went inside to gather my things.

As I shoved my rifle into the scabbard, I looked across the saddle at Lora and the kids

109

standing under the arbor over the front gate. It wasn't easy to just ride off and leave them.

"Now, I'll be gone for a few days. You kids be good and do what Lora tells you, OK?"

Sarah nodded her head earnestly.

Jacob spoke clearly. "Yes sir."

Stepping around Dusty, I wrapped Lora in my arms and we locked eyes for a moment, then I kissed her.

"John, not in front of the children!" She scolded me playfully.

The kids were giggling.

"Baby, I'll kiss you in front of God and everybody. I'm off, but I shouldn't be gone more than a week."

"Becky will be here later today, and Tom will join us for supper. They'll stay with us till you get back. Stay safe and hurry home, darling."

"I always hurry home to you, Baby."

I turned and mounted Dusty. With a final wave, I turned him and we trotted away across the bridge over Bear Creek.

DAN ARNOLD

THE ROCKING M ~
BUTTERCUPS AND OLD BILL

10.

The wagon road we followed south wasn't really a road at all. It had never been graded and was basically just the ruts made by years of wagon traffic across ground that was the easiest way to travel to and from Bear Creek, from farms and ranches to the south. I suspected the road was situated across land which was technically all private property and none of this land belonged to the state or the county.

Just south of Bear Creek, within two or three miles, we passed a few small farms, after that the country became much more

113

sparsely populated. I noted there was no barbed wire down this way.

Occasionally I would see a stack of rocks, like trail sign, at one or the other edge of the road. I figured the stacked rocks probably marked a boundary of someone's land.

The road wound around, twisting and turning to avoid the steep hills and deep water crossings. It also had to meander to avoid rock outcroppings and precipitous arroyos. Dusty covered the distance in about three hours. In all that time, we didn't meet a single wagon or any people coming north.

As we approached the back side of Yellow Butte, I was enthralled by how pretty this country was. The buttes and mesas rose up here and there like flat topped mountains. Most were only a few hundred feet higher than the surrounding country. It was as if they

114

were mountains in training, or mountains that'd never quite gotten to the point.

Some began as a gently sloping hillside and then leveled off, with crags and cliffs on two or three sides. Most of them were heavily forested on the top, with pines and spruce in abundance. Some looked like giant cakes or biscuits dropped onto the foothills. Others looked a little like castles, with great rocky promontory towers of a few hundred feet.

The land along the edges below the elevated plateaus was scattered with huge slabs of granite or sandstone, showing through the brush and grass, with here and there a few trees, most of which were close to streams coming out of the mountains.

I don't know much about geology, but the buttes and mesas appeared to be hard high ground that'd been left exposed after a

115

tremendous runoff from some ancient sea or the great flood had washed away surrounding land.

Maybe I was just hungry, but I couldn't get the thought of cakes and biscuits to go away.

I decided to leave the road at a place where it curved down and away toward the town of Buttercup and ride on up to the top of Yellow Butte. I could see that climbing up the shoulder, from the north side, was the easiest way to get to the top. Yellow Butte had ragged cliffs on the sides facing south, east and west.

I scouted around on Dusty and eventually found a little used trail that would take us up onto the mesa.

About thirty minutes later, we were up on the top of Yellow Butte, riding through pristine, old growth forest, with no sign that

116

men had ever been here. We crossed through a small meadow where there was a lot of deadfall timber, went back into the tress, and eventually emerged from a stand of aspen, several hundred feet above Buttercup Creek, high on the south rim of Yellow Butte.

From this vantage point at the top of Yellow Butte, I had a good view of the surrounding country. Behind me, the forest blocked my view to the north, but I could see for miles to the south, across rolling hills, and the occasional obstruction of another mesa. Mostly, I saw brushy grassland with small stands of pine and poplar. Here and there, and for as far as the eye could see; cattle were scattered individually and in small groups.

In far distant and widely separated locations, I thought maybe I could see some ranch buildings. Farther away still, the great wall of the Front Range jutted out here and there, like the teeth of a saw blade, in shades of blue and purple, with glacier ice on the tops of the highest peaks, seen through the softening effect of dozens of miles of atmosphere.

To the east, the land fell away like stair steps, down onto the plains, but just a few miles away in that direction, I could see the town of Buttercup.

To the west, Buttercup Creek meandered out of the towering heights of the Rocky Mountains, six or seven thousand feet above me, flowing out of the high country between other buttes and mesas like this one. As my eyes followed the meanders of the creek, back to the base of Yellow Butte, I saw far below me, a house, barn, and livestock pens, with no signs of life or activity.

I turned Dusty back the way we had come, and started looking for a trail that would take us down to the ranch buildings below.

There were several game trails which might've served, but I needed one I could be sure was suitable for a horse and rider. Jacob had told me he'd been up on the mesa with his dad, so I knew there would be a fairly direct route somewhere nearby.

Shortly, I saw a break in the brush and trees off to our right, so I turned Dusty that way, and soon found what I was looking for.

There was a natural cleft in the face of the mesa wide enough for a man on horseback to ride into. Over the centuries, the bottom of the cleft had been filled with broken rock and dirt and had become a natural but narrow trail down the face of the mesa between walls of solid rock, to the grassland below. I imagined not many years ago only the Indians knew of this trail, and before them, only the native animals.

It took us the better part of thirty minutes to work our way down the narrow and steep defile. Sometimes, a stirrup would scrape the rock on one side or the other, but we eventually came out into a thick stand of brush and scrub oak, with huge slabs of fallen rock all around us. When we emerged from that, we were at the edge of a cleared yard, surrounding the same house I'd seen from the top of the mesa. I could hear the creek flowing somewhere on the other side of the house, and smell the cottonwoods growing there.

The house was a simple, single story, weather beaten, pier and beam style ranch house, with glass in the windows. It had a tin roof which also provided a covered porch all the way around it.

RIDING FOR THE BRAND

I rode Dusty around the house, and down to the edge of the creek where I dismounted to let him drink. I tied him to a big cottonwood limb there in the shade, and walked back up to the house.

I stopped in the front yard for a moment and looked around.

Although it was obvious people had once lived here, there was no sign of life.

The vegetable patch was all dead and dried up. Even the weeds, which had found a foothold in some places, were dead.

It was evident no one had been here for some time.

There is a strange lonely feeling about abandoned buildings, as though it is unnatural for them to be empty. Cemeteries are just as quiet, but they seem to be somehow more restful and less lonely. Maybe that's because cemeteries are anything *but* empty. Did you

121

ever wonder why they put fences around cemeteries? The people on the outside are in no hurry to get in there, and the people on the inside aren't trying to get out.

A ranch like this was meant to be a thriving and lively place, with chickens in the yard, laundry drying in the breeze, livestock in the pens, and people doing chores. There should've been children laughing and playing hide and go seek, cattle lowing, maybe even someone fishing in the creek.

I was alone here, except for Dusty and the occasional bird darting through the trees.

This was a beautiful location, with the ranch buildings facing Buttercup Creek, surrounded by trees, and Yellow Butte rising majestically above and behind it. Across the creek, viewed through and above the pussy willows lining the banks, was rolling grassland

From my position in the yard, I could see into the empty barn and pens.

I thought of what a great place this must have been for Jacob and Sarah, when both of their parents had still been alive.

That thought brought me back to why I was there.

I walked up on the porch, and even though I knew no one would answer, I knocked on the front door.

I little gust of wind kicked up some dust in the yard, and swirled it away in the vortex of a dust devil.

I pushed open the door of the house, not knowing what to expect.

Often, when structures are abandoned, wildlife moves in. I knew I might find a family of raccoons in the cupboards, owls in the rafters, or rattlers under the furniture.

I was hoping not to find the remains of Mrs. Murphy, somewhere in the house.

I looked in every room.

All of the furnishings were still in place. There were braided rugs on the floor, curtains and pull shades at the windows, even beds in the two bedrooms, a big bed in one room, and bunk beds in the other. The beds had been stripped, but the horse hair mattresses were still there. I found crockery and cookware in the cupboards, but there was no coffee, or any of the other staples. There were no food items of any kind, anywhere in the house, nothing that might attract animals or insects.

I found the house neat and tidy. There was some dust on the furniture, but it appeared the house had been cleaned and readied for someone to come back to. There was even firewood stacked by the stove and kerosene in the lamps.

I wondered who had gone to the trouble, and what had become of Mrs. Murphy's body.

I sat at the table and considered the situation.

When their mother died, Jacob and Sarah had turned the milk cow loose, and started walking the long miles to Bear Creek, barefoot, with no supplies or money.

It was a fifteen mile hike as the crow flies, longer if you followed the road. Those kids had started walking barefoot, across unfamiliar country, to get to a city where they didn't know anyone.

Why hadn't they just gone to a neighboring ranch, or walked the few miles downstream, to the little town of Buttercup?

I heard horses approaching, so I walked out on the porch to meet the riders.

11.

Two men on horseback stopped in the yard.

To my surprise, one of the men was "Snake" Flanagan. I'd met Snake in Amarillo. He was said to be a gunfighter, once upon a time, but we had never had a reason to lock horns. He and I were both about fifteen years older since last we met, but I hoped I'd aged better than he had. Snake had never been tall, but now he appeared thin and shrunken.

The other man was much bigger, and he appeared angry. He got off his horse and stormed up onto the porch.

"Mister, you're trespassing on private property. What're you doing here? We don't cotton to strangers around here." He informed me as he loomed over me.

"I have friends who used to live in this house. This is their land. I'm just having a look around. Who are you, and why are you here?" I asked.

"My name is Higgins, and this is my place now."

I shook my head.

"Not according to the deed records in the county courthouse in Bear Creek. This land belongs to the Murphy heirs."

"You're a damn liar. Who might you be, when you're at home?" Higgins asked, with a sneer.

He stood so close, his foul breath nearly knocked me over.

"My name is John Everett Sage, whether I'm at home or here on this porch."

"I don't care who you are. You leave now, or I'll dump your body in the outhouse."

I took a long slow breath. Was that what had become of Jacob and Sarah's mother? Had her body been dumped in the outhouse?

Something inside me turned to stone, and anger like a flame began spreading through me.

"Careful Higgins, he's just as likely to kill you as not," the man called 'Snake' said. "He's a dangerous gunman from way back. You may have read about him in the newspapers."

"Phaw!" spat Higgins, "Them papers tell stories so's folks will buy um. Fancy suit and all, he don't look like nothing to me."

He reached for his gun.

I was close enough to whip my gun out and smash it across his face, even as his gun came free of the holster.

Higgins crumpled, his gun was flung aside. I turned on Snake, leveling my Colt.

Snake Flanagan sat his horse calmly, and slowly lifted both hands.

"Not my fight, Sage," he grinned. "...watch your back now."

Higgins came up off the floor of the porch, quicker than I could believe. Before I could swivel fully around, he slammed into me like a run-away locomotive.

I was driven backward into a corner post of the porch. The impact knocked my gun out of my hand, the air out of my lungs, and we both crashed through the post and down into the yard.

Higgins landed on top of me, effectively keeping me from catching my breath. I was trying to shake the cobwebs out of my head and get some air, when I remembered Higgins was trying to kill me. He was a scrapper and a brawler, and he outweighed me by nearly a hundred pounds. His hands clamped around my throat, and my world began to get very small.

The sound of my hideout Colt Lightening .38 being cocked, made him stop squeezing my throat. The pressure of the barrel up under his chin made him rise up off me, as though he were being lifted by a block and tackle.

"I told you, Higgins. He's a gun slick from way back. Man like that don't kill easy." Snake observed.

There was a huge welt swelling over Higgins' right eye, from where my .45 had clipped him.

"You could have backed my play, you sum'bitch." Higgins growled at Snake Flanagan.

"I told you not to start a fight with him, you done that all on your own." Snake responded.

I pushed Higgins backward with my gun, until we reached where my .45 had landed in the yard.

I knew I would never be able to get him to Bear Creek by myself, at least not without having to kill him. He would try to jump me the first chance he got.

"You wouldn't kill an unarmed man would you?" He asked

"Higgins, you're just as dangerous with or without a gun. I expect you would have no qualms about killing me if *I* was unarmed. Now, back up over there toward your partner, so I can watch you both at the same time."

When he was far enough away, I picked up my .45, and with both guns leveled on the two men, I decided to let them go. But Higgins had something to say.

"You just bought yourself a one way ticket to hell, mister." He said.

"I don't anticipate that outcome, but I suspect *you* will most likely end up there."

"Oh, we'll meet again, alright. Maybe Jud Coltrane will let me peel your hide, and nail it to the barn door."

"Well then, maybe I should just kill you now, and save myself the trouble."

Higgins paled.

"Whoa there, Sage, if you do, I'll have to mix in myself." Snake said.

"Is that right? Are you feeling lucky, Snake? Do you think you could pull your gun faster than I can shoot both of you?"

Snake shrugged.

"It's up to you." He said.

I nodded.

"OK, Higgins this is your lucky day. Get on your horse and get out of my sight. If you try something like this again, I'll put a bullet through the pimple on your shoulders you call your head."

Higgins looked relieved, as he mounted his horse. Then he remembered something.

"What about my gun?" He asked.

"It's my gun now. Be grateful I took it, instead of your life."

Snake Flanagan looked amused.

"Thanks for staying out of this, Snake." I said.

"Por nada. When I'm ready, we'll see just how good you really are."

"...Another time, another place." I said.

"You won't have long to wait." He replied.

I watched them both ride away. When they were completely gone from sight, or sound, I holstered my .45, put my .38 back in the shoulder holster, tucked Higgins gun behind my belt, and retrieved my hat.

The yard didn't seem quite as lonely as when I had first arrived.

I walked down to the creek to get Dusty. It was time for us to go into Buttercup.

DAN ARNOLD

12.

Buttercup wasn't much of a town. There was a general store that served as post office, stage stop, and feed store. Across the road was a dingy, little saloon. Some horses were tied at the hitching rail in front of the saloon. On the other side of the plank bridge across Buttercup Creek, there was a small livery stable and stock yard. Those and a couple of frame houses, some shacks and outhouses, were about all there was to Buttercup.

I stepped off Dusty in front of the general store and left him ground tied, with the reins draped across the hitching rail.

Inside, I was surprised to see how tidy and well organized the establishment was. A quick look around showed canned goods, bolts of fabric, tools and harness, guns and ammo, even ladies garments on display in separate sections of the store.

From behind a glass counter with a small assortment of glassware, china and silver on display, a bald headed man wearing an apron said, "Good morning, sir. Welcome to Buttercup."

"Morning," I nodded in response.

"How can we help you, sir? I don't believe we've seen you in here before." The man said.

"I was wondering if you might be able to tell me something about some folks who used to live here. Also, do you have any fresh bandages?"

"...Bandages? Are you hurt?"

138

"I think I broke open a wound. I've just had the stiches out."

"Lida! Come quick, we have an injured man in here," he called.

"Oh, there's no need for that, I can manage..."

A heavyset woman with gun metal grey hair pinned up in a bun, came bustling through a doorway at the back of the store.

"Nonsense!" she snapped at me. "We'd better have a look at it, dontcha know?"

"Now Lida, maybe the gentleman isn't comfortable having a lady fussing over him," the storekeeper observed.

"No, it's not that..."

"Then we'll see to it now, by golly." She nodded at me, with a stern look.

"Yes ma'am." I said.

I've been learning to pick my battles.

I took off my suit coat and when I did, my badge and guns were clearly on display outside my waistcoat.

"Yumpin yiminy! He's a lawman!" she exclaimed.

"Yes, ma'am, I'm the Sheriff of the county."

"Sheriff Sage? Are you Sheriff Sage?" The man asked.

"Yes sir. I don't believe we've met. Who do I have to thank for your kindness?"

"I'm Henry Burke and this is my wife, Lida Burke. This is our store."

"...Pleased to meet you folks."

"Where are you hurting, Sheriff?" Mrs. Burke asked.

I shrugged out of my shoulder holster, unbuttoned my waistcoat and gently eased out of it. I could feel my shirt stuck to my back, where I'd been bleeding. I carefully lowered my leather braces, and began unbuttoning my shirt. I'd taken off my tie and celluloid collar as soon as I left the abandoned ranch.

"Tssk, tssk, tssk. Don't take your shirt off, yet. I'll getcha a warm cloth and we'll soak it loose first." Mrs. Burke instructed me. "Then I'll be washing the shirt. Nice white shirt like that. Tssk, tssk, tssk." She headed out through the back doorway.

"What happened to you, Sheriff?" Mr. Burke asked me.

"I got in a tussle with a pretty good sized fella, fell off the porch and landed on my back in the yard. I guess I opened up the bullet wound."

"This is rough country. You might not want to be riding around in your Sunday best," he observed."

He had a point. I should've put on trail clothes before I left Bear Creek. I'd gotten

141

used to life in the city where my appearance needed to be more formal.

"Have you got anything more suitable, in my size?" I asked him.

"Sure do. Cowboys around here get most of their gear from us. Let's see, you'll need some britches, a shirt, a work vest and a jacket. I've got a good canvas jacket just your size. Anything else you need?"

"Yep, I'll need some Arbuckle's, beans, salt pork, some canned goods...."

"Are you planning on being around for a spell?"

"Now, papa, don't you be a buttin' in to this man's business." Mrs. Burke said, coming back with a bowl of hot water, bandages and what not.

"I'll be staying out at the Murphy place for a couple of days."

"Uhh, Sheriff, it's not my place to tell you what to do, but I wouldn't do that if I were you." Mr. Burke said.

"Oh, why's that?"

Mrs. Burke laid a hot wet rag on my shoulder to loosen my shirt. It felt good.

"It's bad business being out there, dangerous too. It's just awful what happened to those folks..."Mr Burke said.

"That's what I wanted to ask you about. Did you know the Murphy's?"

"Oh, yah, you betcha!. Such a nice family. Sad, what happened to em." Mrs. Burke said.

"What happened to them?"

The Burkes exchanged looks.

"I'd rather not say. Best to just let it all go on by." Mr. Burke said.

Mrs. Burke began to gently peel my shirt away from the wound.

"You should tell him, papa. He's the law, don'tcha know? It's about time we had some law and order around here, you betcha!"

"I intend to find out what happened to the Murphy's. It's why I'm here. Any help you can give me will be appreciated."

"Well they hung him, didn't they? …Left a widow and two children, with no one to look out for em. She took it hard, the missus did, and her health wasn't good to begin with. By the time we realized she hadn't been coming for supplies… We buried her next to her husband. I don't know what became of the children." Mr. Burke said, all in a rush.

"He'll be needing a shirt to wear, till this one is clean and dry." Mrs. Burke observed, helping me out of my soiled shirt. "If he's going to be here a spell, he'll need two or three sets of work clothes.."

"Right, I was just about to get him some things."

"Well then, get to it, by golly!" She snapped.

Mr Burke started pulling things from the shelves.

"Wait. Are you saying someone hung Mr. Murphy? Why, and who would do that?"

"Ya, you betcha, they hung him for a rustler. That Jud Coltrane, he runs this country. He wanted the Murphy place, don'tcha know? Well, he said they found Sean Murphy with stolen cattle, so they strung him up and left him to the buzzards and the crows. Me and papa cut him down and took him home to his missus, you betcha. Buried him, too. The poor widow, being too weak and sick to do it, don'tcha know? It was murder, it was."

"Now momma, we don't know that. Maybe Mr. Murphy did steal some cattle."

145

"Phaw," she spat. "That Jud Coltrane is a thief and a liar, papa. You know it yourself, by golly! Sean Murphy never did a bad deed in all the time we knew him. Don'tcha know?"

Mr. Burke hurried back with some denim jeans, a couple of checkered shirts, a four pocket vest and the waxed canvas jacket.

"There's nothing good can come of speaking ill of our neighbors, mamma. The Sheriff here will figure things out on his own. Won't you, Sheriff?" He asked.

"Yes sir. I will. You can count on it."

13.

After she got me all cleaned up, Mrs. Burke didn't think I needed to be bound up with a bandage. She draped some clean gauze over the wound and told me my shirt, braces and vest would hold it in place, and in a day or two I wouldn't need any bandage at all.

"If you don't go falling off porches, don'tcha know?" She said.

Mr. Burke took me in the back of the store so I could change clothes. When I came out, he nodded and said I should have a bandana or two, just in case.

I'd put my badge in a pocket of my new vest and put my gun belt and holsters back on. Once I put the canvas jacket on, neither of my guns were immediately visible.

I arranged to have Mr. Burke take the extra clothes, supplies and some tools out to the Murphy house, while I went across the street to the saloon.

The saloon was pretty basic. As you walked through the swinging doors, the bar was at the far end of the room. Toward the front, there were four tables with four or five chairs at each table. About midway down the right side, between the windows, there was a potbellied stove. On the left side, there was a dusty piano occupying that position. There was an open area down the center of the room between the tables. That was all there was to it. The bar itself was built of plank boards laying on beer barrels, but it had a brass rail and spittoon at each end.

The back wall had a decent mirror reflecting the available light from the windows or the lanterns that were on the

148

walls and hanging from the ceiling. Shelves on both sides of the mirror, displayed the bottled goods. At one end of the bar, a closed door suggested a back room or access to the privy.

Two men were standing at the bar, talking loudly to the bearded bartender. A lone old man with a moustache and long white hair sat at a table with his back to the wall. He was drinking coffee and watching me as I came in. There was no one else inside.

Ordinarily I would have stepped away from the door as I came in, but under the circumstances I just headed straight for the bar.

"Howdy mister," the bartender said. "What'll it be?"

"Coffee and information," I replied.

"Well, the coffee'll cost you a nickel and I ain't got no information."

149

The two cowboys snickered at his answer.

"Must be mighty good coffee." I observed.

"Sure is. Arbuckle's, I buy it across the street. It's all you can drink though."

"…Fair enough." I rapped on the bar top, as I glanced at the cowboys.

They looked back at me, clearly amused and a little bit drunk.

"I see you boys are riding horses with the Rocking M brand. That's the Murphy ranch brand isn't it?"

"Is it? We see you're wearing brand new store-bought duds. What happened? Somebody steal your clothes?" one of them asked.

"Something like that. Now answer my question, boys."

"Who do you think you are? We never seen you around here before." The other one said. They were trying to pull themselves together for a fight. They stepped away from the bar, their hands near their guns.

I braced them straight up, pulling my new canvas coat just far enough aside to reveal my .45, sitting cross draw style on my left hip.

To my surprise, the old man sitting at a table behind the drunken cowboys suddenly spoke sharply.

"Hey! Stop right there. You boys don't want to let your mouths lead you down a one way trail. You'd better answer his question and ride on out of here. Cain't you see, this man is a lobo wolf. He don't bark, he just bites."

These men weren't gun hands. They were just day rate cowboys. The younger of the two was no more than eighteen years old. With me in front of them and the old man behind them, they didn't want any part of a fight.

The older cowboy decided to talk.

"We ride for the Bar C Bar, that's the Coltrane outfit. Bet you've heard of it."

"I've heard of it. Why are you riding Rocking M horses, if you ride for the Bar C Bar?

"They come with the job, part of the cavvy. What's it to you?"

"I ride for the Rocking M."

The two cowboys looked at each other.

"Listen Mister, we don't know nothin' about that."

"I figured as much. You ride on back to the Bar C Bar and tell your boss, I expect to see a bill of sale for those horses. You understand a bill of sale?"

"We know what it is, but you got no right to ask for one."

"I do. You tell him I want it, or I'll be asking you why you didn't. Now, are you going to walk out of here, or be dragged out?"

They practically tripped over each other scrambling for the door.

I walked over to the table where the old man was sitting.

"Mind if I sit down?"

"Free country," he said.

He was wiry and tough, the way old men get who live on the land. Part steel and part jerked beef. He had a drooping white mustache covering his lips, stained brown by tobacco or coffee. His eyes were bright and alert in lids creased and wrinkled by sun and time. His hands were folded on the table, hands of leather, strong and scarred. He sat calmly and regarded me without expression.

His large brimmed sombrero hung on his back from a plaited horsehair stampede string. He wore a bright red bandana over a faded blue shirt and a dark grey wool vest. The bandana held at the neck by a sterling silver ring with a single turquoise stone in it. His thinning hair was long, falling nearly to his shoulders, and as white as his mustache.

"Do you know me?" I asked him.

"I know yer kind, same as me. Them boys was a little liquored up. They was fixin' to make a stupid mistake. What's yer handle, son?"

"John. You?"

""John, huh? No last name? Alright, John, some call me Scout, others, other things. You can call me Bill."

"You been around here long, Bill?

"Nope, at least not lately. I was in these parts some time back, just passing through now."

I nodded.

"Same with me. The first time I was in this part of the country was right after the war between the states. I pushed a herd through here with Charlie Goodnight. It's all different now." "Hmmm," he said, regarding me with narrowed eyes..

The bartender brought me a cup and set the coffee pot on the table. He left without saying a word. I poured coffee in my cup and looked at the old man. He nodded his answer, so I poured some in his cup, too.

The old man picked up his coffee cup with both hands and looked over the top at me.

"You're part right and part wrong about the thing you said, John. The land don't change. The landmarks pretty much stay the same. Injuns say, 'Only the rocks live forever'. Times change, but the land don't. There're more people now, though.

"Reckon so. More people, but not better."

"I reckon we're all just passing through. You said you ride for the Rocking M?"

"That's right."

"I've seen Rocking M cattle scattered all over the range. Why is that?"

I thought about it. How should I answer? Could I trust this old man?

"There's been no one around to tend to the ranch for some time."

"Why's that?"

"Well, Bill, the Murphys are dead. The children are safe, but the ranch hasn't been worked in weeks. I just got here, today."

"The old man set his jaw, his mouth shrinking into a narrow slit, again disappearing under his mustache.

"Did you know the Murphys?" I asked.

"I knew Sean Murphy."

We sat in silence until he felt like telling me his story.

"I first come west through the Republic of Texas about fifty years ago. After the war with Mexico, in '48, I scouted with Fremont and Carson with the blessing of President Polk. There were damn few white men in this country then, plenty of Indians though. I was in California with Fremont in '49. I always had the itch to see new country, so I guided wagon trains, and roamed all over, from St Louis to San Francisco. I fought with Carson in New Mexico, during the big war you spoke of. When I first came through here, about thirty years ago, I was prospecting.

157

It was me named Buttercup Creek. I staked a claim on a couple sections of land on the edge of the mountains, just west of Yellow Butte, with Buttercup Creek running right through the middle of it, thinking I would make a ranch here one day."

It suddenly dawned on me I was talking to the legendary frontier scout, Indian fighter, and wagon master, Rupert William "Old Bill" Kennemer. I hadn't realized who he was. I remembered the deed to Murphy was from "R.W. Kennemer". I hadn't made the connection. Like most folks, I'd heard of him, but I figured he was long since dead.

"Why did you call it Buttercup Creek? I haven't seen any Buttercups."

Bill chuckled.

"Buttercups is poison to cattle and horses. I figured the name would keep cow men away from it, till I was ready to build my ranch. Well, the years go by and things don't always go the way you think they will," he observed. "I was scouting for the army over in Arizona territory about fifteen years back. This young Lieutenant named Murphy saved my hair. We became friends and he told me he was sick of the desert country and wanted to get out of the army and build a ranch somewhere with good water and mountain views. I was headed for Mexico and I decided to sell him some of my land in Colorado territory. I deeded him a section and a half, keeping a half section for myself. We were to be partners in the ranch, if he could make it work."

"I believe he did that." I said.

"Hell yes, he did. Sean had a head for business and he weren't afraid of work. He got him a fine wife, a couple of kids, and he built us a herd. Got near wiped out one

159

winter, a few years back. Altogether, it took him more than ten years to really turn a profit. He wrote me and said I should come see the place. Why I'm here."

"Did you know he was dead?"

The old man lowered his head.

"No," he said. "I just got here myself."

The old man pulled a bone colored pipe with a silver mounted stem and a tobacco pouch out of a vest pocket. He tamped tobacco into the bowl and popped a match, lighting the pipe. He sat and smoked while I sipped my coffee.

"What will you do now," I asked.

"We'll see... You say you ride for the Rocking M. What's all this to you?"

"A few weeks ago I found two little kids, Jacob and Sarah Murphy, hiding in the barn at the livery stable up in Bear Creek. My wife and I took them in. Jacob is six and

Sarah is four years old. At first they couldn't or wouldn't talk about what happened. We didn't know who they were or where they came from. Over time, we were able to get bits and pieces of the story. We learned that both of their parents were dead. I did some research and found the deed you spoke of. I decided to ride down here and see if the kids have any family in the area. I found the ranch abandoned, and I had a little run in with a local tough who claimed it was his place now..."

"...He still there?" The old man interrupted, coldly.

"No, I ran him off. I came on here to get some supplies over at the general store. They told me what happened to the Murphy's."

He looked at me, waiting to hear what had become of his friend and partner.

161

"Bill, someone lynched Sean Murphy, for rustling…"

"…That's a damned lie. Sean would never steal another man's cattle." Bill said, slapping his hand on the table.

"I understand. Even if it were true, lynching is illegal. Whoever is responsible will be brought to justice."

"Damned right they will, and mighty soon," he agreed.

I didn't like his tone. I could tell he figured to be the one to administer justice, his own brand of justice.

"I was told Mrs. Murphy had been ill for some time and the death of her husband was more than she could bear. She died shortly after he was killed. The folks over at the general store saw to both burials."

"I owe um for that." Bill observed.

"They seem like good folks. Their name is Burke, Henry and Lida Burke. When they heard Mr. Murphy had been lynched, they went out and retrieved his body and buried it at the ranch. Sometime later, when they realized Mrs. Murphy hadn't come in for supplies, they went out to the ranch and found her dead. They buried her beside her husband. By then, the children had walked all the way to Bear Creek."

Old Bill put away his pipe.

"Seems like you told me near all I need to know. I'm obliged to you for taking in Sean's kids. They ain't got nobody else. You go on home to your wife and take care of those children, John. I'll do what needs to be done here."

"No, I'm staying. I've had supplies sent out to the ranch. You're welcome to join me there."

163

"The ranch is half mine, and none of yours." He said.

"That's right. I'm representing the owners of the other half, Jacob and Sarah."

He nodded thoughtfully. "It'll take some work to put things right."

"Two heads are better than one and many hands make light work." I quoted.

He nodded again.

"So I've heard

"So you'll throw in with me out at the ranch?"

"It might go that way. I'll be along, directly. I want to ride around and see what I see." Bill said, standing up.

He wore striped pants tucked into high moccasins with rawhide soles, a Colt revolver rested casually in his waistband. He was holding the rifle that had been laid across his lap as we talked.

RIDING FOR THE BRAND

I found myself staring at the rifle. The old man, seeing my interest, spoke up.

"Christian Sharps, Creedmoor rifle. This un's a .45 caliber breechloader. She's accurate out to at least a thousand yards. You ever et antelope?"

I whistled.

"That's more than a half mile. Naturally, I've seen many a Sharps carbine or rifle, and the Remington version of them. I've heard of Creedmoor and the sharpshooting contests, but I've never seen one of those rifles rigged like that before. The engraving is beautiful."

"You won't likely see another."

"Are those sights adjustable?"

"Yep, windage and elevation, front and back. Peep sights the thing."

We walked outside to the only horse still tied in front of the saloon. It was a

165

spotted horse with a silver worked saddle and bridle. The heavy Spanish spade bit was silver as well. The horse also wore a pencil bosal, He was secured with a neck rope and not tied by the bridal reins.

"Hackamore man, huh?" I asked.

"Yep, picked it up in California from the vaqueros, only way to train a bridle horse."

"I know what you mean. I've spent some time in California myself.

He looked over at Dusty, where he stood untied at the hitching rail across the street.

"Injun pony? He looks mountain bred." Bill observed.

"He is that."

Bill untied the neck rope and draped it around his saddle horn. He stepped up on the spotted horse and pulled his sombrero up on his head, shading his face and eyes. He snugged up his stampede string as he held the Creedmoor rifle across the pommel of his saddle. Without saying another word he turned his horse and trotted off across the plank bridge, leaving me standing in the street.

DAN ARNOLD

14.

I approached the ranch more carefully this time.

When I came to a place where there was a pile of stones marking the property line, I swung wide and started looking the property over. I topped a rise and saw below me fence posts forming the start of a very long fence line.

Clearly, Sean Murphy had started to fence his land.

It wasn't common to see vast areas of unfenced ranch land anymore. To help keep livestock off the tracks, the railroads were fenced with barbed wire, down both sides.

Most of the farmers and ranchers had gone to fencing their land with barbed wire. I saw it in Texas and it was becoming the norm

169

here in Colorado as well. This open range land was becoming scarce, especially where all of the land was privately owned. The days of free grazing and wide open spaces were coming to an end.

In the early days of ranching it was all open range. One man's cattle would graze beside another's. There would be big roundups a couple of times a year, where the cattle would be sorted, counted and new calves would be branded by the representatives of the various outfits. Apparently they were still doing it here, but Murphy had decided to fence his land.

Was that what had gotten him killed?

From the rise I surveyed the country all around me. It was good grassland with cattle scattered in clusters. Most of them wore the Bar C Bar brand, with here and there a

Rocking M or another brand mingled in. There was no sign of riders.

I rode down to the deceptively named Buttercup Creek and rode along it until I came to a good place to cross. Where it narrowed there was good deep water and wherever it widened out it sang and laughed across the rocks and pebbles.

If there was this much steady water, this late in the year, I wondered what would happen when the spring thaw sent melted snow water down the creek.

Shortly, I found a cut bank where cattle had been crossing at one of the wide shallower places.

A single section of land is six hundred and forty acres. The Rocking M, being two sections of land, was twelve hundred and eighty acres, not a big ranch by most standards. The thing that made it special was the location. The soil here supported good grass, the creek was constant and accessible and there were some scattered trees and natural shelter afforded by the terrain. All in all, great cattle land. Because the ranch was on the edge of the mountains, it had access to high mountain meadows with nutrient rich grass-free for the taking–if you could get to it. For the cattle on the Rocking M it could be done with a single day's drive. Properly managed, this ranch could hold four or five hundred head and still be able to make hay.

The bigger ranches were generally bigger because there was less grass and water available. A fifty thousand acre ranch might only be able to hold a thousand head of cattle. In dry country, even less, and there would be no hay produced.

Old Bill had recognized all of that when he staked his claim here. Murphy had worked at building the ranch and the herd. If he had finished fencing it, he would have controlled the best grass and water for miles around. He could have better managed his breeding program and protected and fed his stock in harsh weather. He couldn't do any of that with his cattle scattered and mixed in with other cattle all over the range.

The sun was getting low in the sky and the air had begun to cool as I approached the ranch buildings. I'd ridden along the edge of the creek and came up to a little hill that afforded a view of the house and barn.

This was where I found the graves.

Sean Murphy and his wife Angela Murphy were laid to rest side by side, the graves covered with stones brought up from the creek. Someone had taken the time to burn the names into boards that formed simple wooden headstones.

I waited up on the little cemetery hill, watching the buildings for a while to be sure there was no one waiting to surprise me as I rode in. There was no sign of life. I'd been hoping Bill and his big, spotted Appaloosa horse would be there.

Shortly, Dusty and I went down the hill and up into the ranch yard. It was dusk now, the time of long shadows. I left him ground tied as I went into the barn to check it out. Inside there were four standing stalls on one side and three box stalls at the back. At the front was a big open area that would hold a couple of large wagons or other equipment, but there was nothing here now. There was no harness for the horses that were no longer here. There was no blacksmith equipment either, not even an anvil. The barn had been stripped of every piece of useful gear that could be hauled off.

I climbed the ladder into the loft and was surprised to find it filled with hay! Back on the ground, I led Dusty into a corral at the side of the barn where there was a trough of water, now growing greenish with algae. Just outside the pen was a hand pump and spigot set to pump water into the end of the trough where it stuck through the fence. No bucket though. I'd thought to buy one of those, and I hoped to find it with the other supplies in the house.

I unsaddled Dusty and turned him loose in the corral. The water would be good enough to get him through one night. Tomorrow, I'd drain and clean the troughs, but I'd need the bucket if I wanted to refill the troughs in the other corrals. I wished I had a good cotton hose, one of those rubberized ones. You could buy them at the hardware store in Bear Creek, but they weren't available at the general store in Buttercup.

Leaving my saddle and bridle in the barn on the side of one of the standing stalls, I climbed into the loft and kicked some hay down to Dusty.

As the sun disappeared behind the mountains, I took my rifle and bedroll and headed for the house.

I stopped on the porch, listening to the stillness of the evening. Somewhere, a coyote howled.

Once inside, I fumbled around in the dark until I got a lamp lit. Eventually I had a fire going in the cook stove and made myself some supper. After I cleaned up my cooking mess, I went out and sat on a bench on the porch, relaxing to the sound of the creek and the other peaceful sounds of the evening.

RIDING FOR THE BRAND

Back inside, I put my handguns under a pillow on one of the beds, took off my boots, turned out the lamps and rolled up in my bedroll. As I started to fall asleep, I heard a lone owl hooting in the night. The Indians say if you hear an owl call your name, it's a portent of your death. I guess he didn't call my name, because I fell into a deep and peaceful sleep.

I woke up a little disoriented, thinking for a moment I was in my bed at home, and I reached out for Lora, before I remembered where I was.

The sun was just coming up in the east. I pulled on my boots and fired up the cook stove. I used the hand pump mounted above the sink and splashed cold water in my face and got the coffee started. Then, after checking and holstering my guns, I went out to check on Dusty. He seemed pleased to see me and appeared to be quite comfortable in his present environment. There was a bit if a chill to the early morning air, reminding me fall was pretty much on us and the first snowfall was only a few weeks away.

After breakfast, I started taking an inventory of the things that would be needed to get through the winter. I wouldn't be here at the ranch then, but hopefully by then we would have restored the ranching operations and someone would be living here. I figured the first order of business would be the fall roundup and I needed to find out when and where that would be.

I'd have to hire some cowboys to help with the roundup, gather the Murphy cattle after the sorting and then drive them here to the ranch. The fence needed to be finished, so the Murphy herd would no longer drift all over the range.

I was reminded I had no idea how many cattle Murphy had. That was the dilemma. What had happened to the equipment and other property stolen from the Murphy ranch? Would I have to sell the cattle to pay for equipment and a fence, which wouldn't be needed to hold the cattle I'd sold to pay for it?

It was time to do some investigating.

DAN ARNOLD

15.

"Cowboys, Sheriff Sage? If there's one thing we used to have plenty of around here it was men and boys who know how to work cattle. What do you need cowboys for?" Mr. Burke asked.

"Do you know if or when they're planning the fall roundup?"

"Course, I've sold supplies to the cooks stocking the chuck wagons. Always try to beat the snow. Roundup starts in two days. That's Friday, day after tomorrow."

"Who all will be involved? I mean how many ranches?"

Mr. Burke scratched his chin. He was thoughtful for a moment.

"I don't rightly know. Time was there would've been several, now though, not so many."

"Why is that?"

Mr. Burke turned away, trying to busy himself with something.

"I asked you why there won't be as many ranches represented at the roundup."

"You tell him, Papa, by golly!" Mrs. Burke said, shaking her finger at her husband.

"Alright, Mama, I'll tell him."

Mr. Burke looked at me with sad eyes.

"The reason there's less ranches now is because of Jud Coltrane. I expect he's bought out, burned out, or run off most of the other ranchers. He pretty much controls the whole range now. I guess there won't be more than three or four outfits at the roundup. It'll be the Bar C Bar and maybe two or three others he hasn't been able to buy, borrow or steal."

"Where is the headquarters for the Bar C Bar?" I asked.

Mr. and Mrs. Burke looked at each other.

"...Coltrane's place is about three miles east of here, right close to the railroad tracks. Jud Coltrane was some put out when the railroad wouldn't let him cut their fences to put in gates. He owns land on both sides of the tracks, but most all of it is on the east side. His headquarters is up on a hill on this side of the tracks, but he only has a couple of hundred acres over here. The two parts of his land are only connected at the point where Buttercup Creek runs under the tracks. That's the only place he can move his cattle from one side to the other. He has to go under the railroad trestle, because of the barbed wire.

Like I said, the railroad owns the fences and they wouldn't put in gates for him."

"Why is that?"

"Well, the Bar C Bar land is four or five sections, close to three thousand acres, but he overgrazed it real bad the first year he owned it. He put over a thousand head on it, because he figured he had enough water. He paid a premium for those cattle too. He had water, but the grass wasn't enough for so many head. The other ranchers wouldn't let him run his cattle in with theirs on the rangeland this side of the tracks. There was trouble over it.

Before he bought his land and shipped in all those cattle, there was probably less than a thousand head altogether, on the whole range. Over here, closer to the mountains there's more rainfall and better grass. On the other side of the tracks it's drier country, it'll hold only a couple of hundred head or so. Coltrane tried to take over the whole range for miles around. He would have ruined everything and put some of those small outfits out of business.

Sean Murphy wasn't about to let Coltrane take over everything. He it was as organized the other ranches. The ranchers with the better grass and a better understanding of land management banded together to make Coltrane graze his cattle on the east side of the tracks. They pushed Coltrane's cattle to the other side of the tracks and barricaded the opening under the railroad trestle. Then they held it by force of arms.

Coltrane's hands wouldn't fight for him. He threatened to bring in gun hands from Texas. When the railroad got wind of the trouble; they wouldn't even talk to Coltrane about gates. They didn't want any part of the trouble."

"Then what happened?"

"Coltrane was forced to sell off most of his herd, but by then the range on the other side of the tracks was near ruined. Once he got his herd down to a manageable size, the other ranchers let him run his cattle in with theirs on the range over here, but Jud Coltrane isn't a forgiving man. He's spent the last couple of years trying to destroy everybody who was against him. He's pretty much done it too.

Murphy was the thorn in his side. Once Coltrane started overtaking the smaller ranches, Murphy started fencing his own place. Sean figured to pull his cattle in, and run his operation on his own land. With him owning the land on both sides of Buttercup Creek, once his place was fenced off, Murphy would've had control of the meadows in the high country as well."

"But Coltrane wasn't willing to let him?"

"If Murphy had done it, he would've controlled most of the access to Buttercup Creek on this side of the tracks, and the approaches to the mountain meadows."

"Is that what got him killed?"

"Jud Coltrane claimed Sean Murphy stole some of the Bar C Bar cattle and was branding the calves with the Rocking M."

"Was he?"

"I don't know. How could anybody know? Sean never got to finish his fence. There was sure enough Bar C Bar cattle on his land, just as there are Rocking M cattle on Coltrane's land. All the cattle are running together on the range right now. It's the whole reason for the roundups." Burke concluded.

"Do you know how many head the Rocking M has?"

"No sir. That's not something Sean Murphy ever had occasioned to mention."

"Can you tell me who the other ranchers are with cattle on this range?"

"I can tell you who should be represented. Well, let's see. There's the Corkscrew outfit, and the Box Cross. They're south and west of here. Murphy's Rocking M, the Bar C Bar and the Flying W. That last outfit is just to the northeast. I expect those are all that's left now, and I ain't real sure about any of it."

"What other outfits that used to be here, are gone now?"

"Mostly the little ones, Tom Slater's Lazy S, Ace Johnson's Rafter J, the Circle B, and us. We ran cattle here, too."

"What happened to your cattle?"

188

Mr. and Mrs. Burke looked at each other again.

"We sold out. We couldn't be in the fight. We have a good business here and we can't afford to take sides."

"What about the others?"

"…Which ones?"

"The uhh, Lazy S, and the other little outfits."

They looked at each other again.

"Well, the Rafter J cattle all disappeared last winter, between one roundup and the next. The barn at the Lazy S caught fire one night, and the Slater's pulled out the next day. The Barnett's who had the Circle B sold out right after one of their riders was shot."

"Let me guess, they all sold out to Jud Coltrane, for pennies on the dollar."

"No, the Slater's didn't sell out. They just pulled out. The Slater's still own the place, wherever they are. ...The rest of em? Yep, pretty much like you just said."

I nodded.

"Where can I find some cowboys who'll work for day wages and help me organize the Rocking M herd?

"Try the Johnson's, by golly! They hate that Jud Coltrane, you betcha."

"They didn't sell out?"

"No. When their herd disappeared, they became hay farmers, or at least they're trying to be. Johnson was the first to fence off his land. When the Johnsons got put out of the cattle business, Coltrane didn't know Johnson and Murphy had already ordered a ton of wire and posts. The Rafter J went right to work fencing their place and had it mostly done before Coltrane even noticed. Johnson and

190

Murphy were going into the hay farming business together. Johnson has equipment Murphy helped him buy. They would've fenced off both of their places and blocked that whole end of the range. Coltrane's hired thugs keep pulling down parts of Johnson's fence, so the range cattle can graze on their place too."

"Where is the Johnson place?"

"It's right between the Rocking M and the Box Cross. I'll draw you a map."

"Thanks. I need to send a telegram. I don't suppose you know of anyone who'll be going up to Bear Creek any time soon."

"I'll be taking my wagon up there tomorrow. I need to re-stock some of my goods. If that's soon enough, I'll go to the telegraph office for you."

"Yep, I sure would appreciate it."

"Help yourself to pen and paper. You write out what you want and where it's to be sent. I reckon half a dollar ought to cover my time and expense."

"Thank you, Mr. Burke. I'll write the telegram, while you draw me a map of the area. I plan to visit as many of the other ranches as I can, before the roundup starts. I'll start with the Rafter J."

16.

If I'd only ridden over the next hilltop, before I crossed the creek on the previous day, I would've come to the corner of the Rafter J land and found it all fenced.

I turned left along the east fence line and found the ranch entrance about a quarter of a mile farther along. The gate was closed and framed by tall posts with a rafter attached across the top. A letter "J" carved from wood was mounted near the peak.

I found that while it was closed, the gate was not locked. I was easily able to open it and pass through on Dusty, then push it closed, without ever having to dismount. From the front entrance, I had a view downhill to the ranch buildings in the distance. I was pleased that all of the grass I

193

could see was recently mowed and some was still piled into wind-rows to cure. I spotted a wagon and team off in the distance to my left, where there was a crew of men gathering the last rows of freshly made hay.

I turned Dusty along a windrow and we trotted toward the wagon. As I approached, the men all gathered at the wagon which was now nearly fully loaded. I slowed Dusty to a walk. Three of the four young men had rifles pointed at me.

I stopped Dusty and slowly raised my hands.

"Good morning, gentlemen. My name is Sage. I'm looking for Mr. Johnson. Could you tell me where I might find him?"

"Who sent you?" One of the men called.

"I'm a friend of the Burkes and the Murphys." I replied.

194

"There ain't no Murphys around here no more."

"I know it, but I represent the family."

One of the young men lowered his rifle and the others followed suit.

"Step down and state your business, mister."

I looked over the men seeing they looked like they were all related, brothers maybe.

I stepped off of Dusty

"Like I said, I'm looking for Mr. Johnson."

They all grinned at each other.

"That'd be me, and me, and me" Three of them replied. "Me too," said the youngest one, chiming in from up in the driver's seat.

I chuckled at that.

"I'm here representing the Murphy outfit. The round up starts the day after tomorrow. I need hands to help with the sorting and branding. Eventually, I plan to move the Murphy herd back on to the ranch proper, once the fence is finished."

"How is it you represent the Rocking M? The Murphys are all dead." The oldest of the four asked. He appeared to be about twenty five years old.

"No sir, not all. The children are still alive, and so is a man named Kennemer. He was Murphy's partner."

They all looked at each other. Then the youngest one, who might have been all of sixteen, shouted. "Hot damn"

"Watch your mouth, Toby." The oldest one said. "Pa hears you swearing like that, he'll whup you, sure as hell."

We all laughed at his joke.

"Where's your dad? I'd like to talk to him."

"He's down at the alfalfa fields. Just ride on down to the house, then follow the spring branch down to the left."

About twenty minutes later, Dusty and I approached what looked to be twenty or thirty acres of harvested alfalfa fields. There were several hay stacks on the edges. I approached three men working around a boxy apparatus made of wood. There was a horse hitched to it.

They watched me with interest as Dusty and I approached.

"Howdy. My name's Sage. I'm looking for Mr. Johnson. The boys up at the front said I could find him down here."

"That'd be me. I'm Horace Johnson. Step down, Mr. Sage. Would you like some cool spring water?"

"No, thank you." I said, as I stepped off of Dusty. "What is that you're working on?"

"It's our hay baler. Broke, I don't suppose you know how to fix it?"

"No, but I've heard you can fix anything with baling wire and spit."

He chuckled. "Yep, I've heard that too. What can we do for you today, Mr. Sage?"

***

When I finished telling him the story, he whistled.

"Say, that's the best news I've heard in a coon's age. Boy howdy, will that ever stick in Coltrane's craw! OK, I've got six sons and three daughters. You'll have me and three of my boys at the roundup. The two older girls can rope and ride as good as many a man, if you want them to help with the herd.

198

Otherwise, they'll handle the chuck. I'll set my other three boys to work on the fence, starting first thing tomorrow. I'll have em get the whole front fenced, clear over to Yellow Butte. Then they'll finish the run down to my corner. They'll get that much done within three or four days. They'll have orders to get it done before the roundup's over.

It may not be pretty, straight, or terribly tight, but it will do, and they'll get it done. We don't need to worry about the rest of the land on the other side of Yellow Butte, till we have more time."

"Uhh, there's a bit of a problem with your offer. Until we sell some of the cattle, I don't have any money to pay for cowboys and hired hands, not to mention fence materials. How many head do you reckon Murphy had?"

"At the last roundup, the Rocking M had well over two hundred head. There'll be

199

something like sixty or eighty new calves by now. There could be as many as three hundred head, maybe more."

I did some quick calculations. At the current price of beef, the Rocking M had nearly two thousand dollars in cattle scattered out on the range. No matter what, I wouldn't need to spend more than a couple of hundred dollars for the most urgent labor and supplies.

"Can you wait to be paid?" I asked.

"Paid for what?" Mr. Johnson asked.

"For all this help you've offered."

"Listen, Sage, for a dozen years Sean Murphy was my neighbor and my friend. We worked side by side when I ran cattle, and he helped me get this hay business started. We bought the fencing materials together. If I can help save the Rocking M, it's the least I can do."

"You understand there may be some risk? When we show up at the roundup, Coltrane or his crew could decide to cause trouble."

"Mister, I ain't never been to a roundup where there weren't no risk of trouble. Your horse can throw you, a cow or bull might gore you to death, or maybe you'll fall and be trampled. Range cattle are unpredictable and so are men. This ain't gonna be no Sunday picnic, no matter how you look at it. We'll be ready for whatever comes at us. You do the same."

"OK. Starting the day after tomorrow, I'd like to gather all the cattle on the Murphy place and push um over to the roundup site. I expect the other ranches will do the same, right?"

"Yep, that's the way it's always been done in these parts."

"I can't provide a cavvy. All the Rocking M horses are gone or scattered. I saw where a couple of the Bar C Bar riders were on Rocking M horses."

"Hmmm. Well, I'm not surprised. Coltrane helped himself to everything Murphy owned that wasn't nailed down. We have horses enough for the first day or so. We'll gather up the Murphy stock at the roundup."

"How did he get away with taking Murphy's property?"

"Coltrane claimed it was all abandoned. I heard he was taking over the whole ranch."

"No, he isn't, and it isn't abandoned. I mean to put things right."

"I'd sure like to see you do it."

"What happened here? How did Coltrane get so powerful?"

Horace Johnson shook his head and kicked at a rock.

"He comes from money. He's a man used to getting what he wants. When we stopped him from ruining the range, he decided to pay us back. He hired some bad men to do his dirty work. I can't prove it, but I know his hired guns threatened Sean Murphy several times. They frightened his wife and kids, something terrible, and I guess you know what happened to Sean?"

"I do."

"There were some riders for other outfits shot at, including two of my boys. One man working for the Barnett's Circle B was shot, nearly killed him. All my cattle just disappeared in six months' time. They burned out the Slater's and ran them off. It's been real bad. After they hung Sean, all the fight went out of most folks. We've all been trying to avoid trouble."

"How many head did you lose?"

"At the fall roundup last year, with our new calves, we had one hundred and fifty-eight head. Over the winter, the boys would come in and tell me they were seeing less and less of our cattle on the range, but I figured my sons weren't real eager to freeze or get shot, and they just weren't scouting hard enough. We always lose a few to the weather, wolves and what not, but at the spring roundup we couldn't find a single animal with our brand on it. No way to know if any of the orphan calves were ours. Sean offered to split his calf crop with us, to give us a fresh start, but I knew it was Coltrane took my herd, or killed um. I knew he wouldn't let me start running cattle again. Sean had bought some haying equipment he was letting me use, including this dad-burn, broke-down baler. I've become a hay farmer. Sean and me planted all this alfalfa the year before the trouble started. Coltrane's men kept pushing cattle in here, hoping to ruin me, but me and my kids would push um out, and we got our fences built. Here lately, the Bar C Bar riders have stopped trying to pull our fences down. I guess the boys and their rifles have discouraged some of that. My boys are itching for a fight. They're mostly growed now. I guess it's time to stand up to Coltrane."

"What about calling in the law?"

"The nearest law is up at Bear Creek. We ain't never had none around here...Wait a minute! Didn't you say your name is Sage? Are you any relation to that Sheriff up there, John Sage?"

"You could say that. You can call me John. Can I call you Horace?"

"Hell no. My friends call me Ace. Put er there, John."

We shook hands.

"One thing, Ace, will you keep it secret I'm the County Sheriff? I want everyone to think I'm just riding for the brand. Can you do that for me?"

Ace chuckled.

"Whoooee, John. I sure will. I can't wait to see the look on Coltrane's face when he finds out!"

17.

My next stop, the Box Cross ranch, was just south of the Rafter J. When I told Ace I was headed there, he cautioned me.

"That's the Cross' place. Them fellers are friendly enough once you get to know em. We've been amiable neighbors, I guess, though they hate the wire. They don't like the way things have gone these last few years, and they hate seeing all the changes.

There are just four brothers living there. Rough as cobs they are. None of their women folk have stayed long. They're drinkers, I believe.

The place never did amount to much, but they still run a couple dozen or so head on the range.

They stayed out of the trouble and never gave Coltrane any reason to harm them. I expect Coltrane figures they're no threat to him. He might be wrong in his thinking."

"Why do you say that?"

"Like I say, they're OK once you get to know um, but it ain't easy. They're a prickly bunch and they stick together. Mean and ornery, I expect if they got riled enough, there would be some killing done. They got no love for Coltrane. If anyone in his bunch crosses one of them, there'll be bloodshed. They won't be interfered with and they won't run.

They've been living off the land since long before I come here, about twelve years ago

When you meet um, you should say I sent you, and don't take offense at um. Like I say, they're rough as cobs and prickly as all get out, but it ain't nothin' personal. They treat each other the same way.

208

Another thing, you might not want to mention you're the law. If you know what I mean."

***

Dusty and I found the trail leading up to their headquarters on the side of a low hill covered in pinõn, scrub pine and brush, with a little creek running by at the base of the hill.

The ranch headquarters turned out to be four little shacks and a run-down barn. Next to the barn were some pole corrals holding half a dozen horses. In front of one of the shacks a gutted mule deer hung from a corner of the porch. I could smell and hear hogs rooting around in a wallow behind the barn.

Before I reached the clearing between the buildings a bearded man stepped out onto his porch. He had a shotgun cradled in one arm and a nearly empty whiskey bottle in his other hand. He whistled and the other men appeared in their doorways, each man similarly bearded and armed.

"Who the hell are you, and what the hell are you doing trespassing on our place?" The older of the four spoke up, loudly.

"My name is John. I'm riding for the Rocking M. Ace Johnson said I should come talk to you boys. Can I step down?"

"Hell no, you can't step down. What do you want?"

"The roundup starts on Friday. I was wondering if you were going to be there."

"That's none of your damn business." Another one of the men spoke up.

"Shut up, Carl. He's talking to me."

"Shut up, your own self, Curt. I'll talk to him if'n I want to."

I decided to carry on.

"The reason I was asking is because I'm new around here and I just wanted to say 'howdy', before we start working cows."

"I heard the Murphy outfit got wiped out." A different man spoke up.

I nodded.

"It nearly did. Sean Murphy and his wife are dead, but their children are safe. Murphy's partner, a man named Kennemer, is somewhere around here.

"Did you say, Kennemer, he any relation to Old Bill Kennemer?" The first man, Curt, asked.

I nodded.

"Himself."

"You're saying Old Bill was Murphy's partner?" The fourth man asked.

"Yep, he still is. Listen, I told you my name, but I don't know yours."

"Well, step down, mister. I'm Curt. These sorry excuses are my brothers, Carl, Ken and Calvin. Folks call us the Cross brothers."

I had to smile, as I stepped off Dusty and shook hands with the rough and bearded men. It was evident none of them had bathed since…maybe ever.

"You got any whisky, Sage?" Calvin asked.

"No. I'm sorry, boys. I'm traveling light."

"Well then, how're we sposed to have a drink, eh?" Kevin asked.

Even out in the fresh air on the edge of the mountains, the smell of the four unwashed men was something terrible.

"Shut up, Kevin. Go fetch a fresh bottle." Curt said.

"You shut up. We're just funnin' with him, Curt."

"Go fetch a bottle or I'll be funnin' with your ugly face." Curt said.

Kevin cut his eyes at me.

"Lucky for you, we make our own 'shine', best corn likker you ever swallered."

He headed for the barn.

Now, I don't have much use for whiskey. On this occasion, I recognized these men were serious about their drinking. These were men who couldn't trust a man who wouldn't take a drink. I figured I could take a drink of their homemade and be on my way.

I was wrong.

I remember the way Dusty looked at me as I tried to climb up into the saddle an hour or two later. He's much smarter than me, he remembered the way back to the Rocking M. I don't even remember getting back.

I woke up in a small pile of hay, on the floor of the barn. Dusty was still saddled. I'd managed to get his bridle off and left it hanging on the saddle horn. He looked at me like I'd let him down—which I had.

I found the sunrise a bit too bright, and every movement caused me pain. I felt nearly sick to death as I unsaddled Dusty and turned him out into his corral.

In the house, I splashed some water into the sink, washed up as best I could, then I fell onto my bed and slept for three or four hours.

I woke up hungry, just before mid-day. I'd intended to ride out to the Flying W, but with the day half gone, I decided to spend the afternoon digging post holes for the fence line. It would do me good to sweat out the poisons.

I vowed never to drink whiskey again.

***

I hate barbed wire. I hate the fences. I miss the days when I could ride from Texas all the way to the frozen north, or west to the Pacific Ocean. As I was growing up with the Romani, we traveled far and wide, seldom bothered by fences. But, those days were gone now, and the Rocking M would have to be fenced.

Dusty and I trotted out to the place where the fence had been started, but never finished. As we approached I saw three young men were hard at work putting in fence posts. I recognized them as being Ace Johnson's boys from the Rafter J. I lifted my hat to set them at ease. Those boys had their rifles near to hand. They'd taken a wagon load of fence posts and dropped them off in a long continuous line that disappeared over a nearby hill.

"Howdy, Mr. Tucker. Pa sent us over to get a jump start on this fence." One of the young men said, as I rode up.

"Looks to me like you've been at it for a spell, I sure do appreciate it."

I stepped off Dusty, took the neck rope out of my saddle bags, and after taking off his bridle I tied him to one of the standing posts with a clove hitch. As I was doing these things the youngster spoke up again.

"Yes sir, we've been working since sun-up."

"You're Toby, aren't you? I remember you from yesterday."

"Yes sir. That's my brother Fred over yonder, and Terry's just beyond him."

"Pleasure," I said. "Toby, I think it's my turn to dig some holes. How're you keeping a straight line?"

"...Mostly dead reckoning. We take a look at a landmark and basically work a straight line toward it. We got us a length of string that'll stretch out to about fifty feet. We take care to look both forward and back to keep the line as straight as possible. The way we've laid out the posts we're pretty near true already. As we get closer, we pick another feature to work toward.

We've been setting about three posts an hour, but I reckon we've slowed down some here lately. This ground through here is mostly rock. We've had to skip several posts in some places. After we stretch the wire, we'll put in some posts with rocks piled around the base wherever we can't put a post in the ground. It ain't pretty, but it'll hold cattle."

"How far is it to the corner of your fence?"

"I figure it's near half a mile. It'll feel like ten miles, though."

I nodded my understanding.

"Well then, let's get to it."

18.

At the end of the day, my shoulder wound was aching. Actually, I was tired and sore all over. My hands were stiff and nearly blistered. I'd only worked half a day, and if I hadn't been wearing gloves, I would've been in trouble. It's funny how soft we can get when we don't work hard every day. Those Johnson boys, on the other hand, had worked like full grown men, from sun-up till the sun went behind the mountains, without much complaint.

Compared to the daily life of a working rancher, life in the city of Bear Creek had made me soft. Of course, I had to allow for the fact I'd been nearly killed a few weeks back. I was just starting to regain my strength.

I figured the roundup was probably going to be pretty taxing.

It was full dark by the time Dusty and I got back to the ranch headquarters under Yellow Butte, now bathed in moonlight. I pulled up short. There were lamps lit inside the house!

I eased off Dusty and left him ground tied by the creek, as I crept up to the house. The shades were all drawn, so I couldn't see inside. I didn't like this. Someone was waiting for me, but who?

I circled wide, away from the house, toward the barn. There in the pen where I'd been keeping Dusty, I found the spotted Appaloosa horse I'd seen Old Bill Kennemer riding. If I had to have a house guest, I figured he's do.

I turned and started across the yard toward the back porch.

"Pleasant evenin' ain't it?" A voice called out from the porch.

I froze in my tracks.

Old Bill Kennemer was sitting on the bench outside the back door. He was hidden in the dark between two windows glowing from the lamps inside. I couldn't see him, but he'd been watching me.

"Yep, it's starting to cool off, though." I said.

"I've got some steaks and taters cooked up inside. Reckon you're hungry. Best come on in and eat."

"Thank you. That'll be as welcome as the rainbow after a thunderstorm."

Old Bill stood up and opened the back door. The light from inside revealed he was still wearing his sombrero and had the Sharps Creedmoor rifle cradled in his arm.

Inside, he kept his rifle but hung his hat down his back with the stampede string holding it in place.

"Go wash up, Sage. I'll fetch your horse from where you left him down by the creek. He'll be wantin' some victuals hisself. There's fresh coffee, if'n you want it."

I pumped water into the sink, and that cold water on my hands and face sure felt good. I scrubbed up as best I could, then swung over to the stove to investigate the good smelling source of onions, potatoes and beef steak coming from that location.

Old Bill came back inside.

"Smart, leaving your horse by the creek. You near snuck up on my Appaloosa in the gloom. You're a careful man." He said, as he set his rifle down, leaning it against the wall by the back door.

"I promised my wife I would be, but I reckon I'm still not as careful as you."

He grinned at me, his dark face turning into all lines and creases under his long white hair.

"I've had me more practice, the reason why I ain't pushing up daisies."

I shrugged, conceding the point.

"How long had you been sitting out there?"

"Oh, not long, I reckon."

"How did you know I'd be coming back here?"

"I seen you out with them young fellers. It was late in the day, so I figured you'd be along, directly. I came on in, and rustled us up some grub. Let's eat."

"You bet, my belly button's rubbing against my backbone. How'd you come to have beef steaks?

Bill grinned and winked.

"This afternoon, I found a steer with a Bar C Bar brand. It'd just been shot."

I figured he was the man who shot it, but I wasn't above eating a good steak.

As we ate, I told him about what I'd learned and seen since we'd met in Buttercup. After a while it dawned on me I was doing all the talking.

"What have you been up to these last couple of days? Will you be joining us at the roundup, tomorrow?"

Old Bill nodded, thoughtfully. He began to pack tobacco into his pipe.

"I'll bed down here, tonight. Tomorrow I'll help you gather and move the cattle on this spread, but I'll drop out before we get to the big roundup. I don't care for crowds. I'll be around though. I'm thinking I might stay on here, if'n it's alright with you."

RIDING FOR THE BRAND

"This ranch is half yours, Bill. You've more right to be here than I do."

He popped a match and lit his pipe.

"Rightee-o then, let's clear up these dishes and get some shut-eye."

Stretched out in my bedroll, I reflected on the day and took some thought for the morrow. I couldn't be sure what would happen at the roundup. My plan was to ride in with Ace Johnson and three of his sons, pushing the cattle we picked up along the way. When we showed up, I intended to claim I was riding for the Rocking M. It was unclear how the sudden appearance of someone claiming to represent the Murphy Ranch would be received.

I didn't fully understand where Old Bill Kennemer fit in to the picture. He was a hard man to read. He seemed more interested in

225

getting whoever had killed Sean Murphy than he was in the ranch itself, but he didn't seem very pleased with my presence on the scene.

I reminded myself of the admonition not to worry about tomorrow-"*Sufficient unto the day is the evil thereof.*" I knew God had a plan and whatever it was, it would be good enough.

With that final thought, I drifted off to sleep.

***

I woke up before dawn, awakened by the sound of Old Bill getting dressed. I met him in the kitchen. While he was slicing bacon for our breakfast I threw some wood on the coals in the stove and got the fire going. When I had the fire well lit, I filled the coffee pot and set it on the stove.

We were saddling our horses in the early light of day, when we heard riders approaching. Bill took his rifle and disappeared back into the dark of the barn. I pulled my rifle out of the scabbard and waited to see who was riding in.

"Hello, the house!" Ace called, as he and three of his older sons pulled up near the back porch.

"Hello, to you." I said. I stepped out from Dusty's off side, placing myself directly behind the riders from the Rafter J.

The four men jumped a little, each showing his surprise.

"Morning, John. Are you expecting trouble?" Ace asked. He and the others turned their horses to face me where I stood with my rifle cradled in my arm.

"Yep, usually. You boys want to step down and drink some coffee before we get started?"

The young men looked like they thought it was be a pretty good idea, but Ace shook his head.

"Naw, we've had breakfast and I figure we should get after it."

Old Bill stepped into the light, easing up beside me.

"Howdy." Ace said.

"Howdy do." Old Bill replied, with a nod.

"You fellers look like you're ready for a fight, which might be a good thing, but are you ready to work cattle?" Ace asked.

"We are" I said." Ace Johnson, shake hands with R.W. Kennemer."

After the introductions were made and everybody had a chance to get the measure of each other, Bill and I mounted up.

"We found twenty four head between here and our place." Ace said. "We pushed them to the edge of the creek. If we spread out from

228

here, we can gather them and whatever else we find on our way to Haystack Rock, where the roundup meets."

"Sounds good to me" I said.

"I'll ride along with you for a spell, but I won't go all the way to Haystack Rock. I expect the five of you can manage without me." Old Bill said.

I looked over at him and asked, "Where you headed?"

He made a forward motion with his hand, ending in a vague gesture.

"Over yonder. I'll be close if you need me."

DAN ARNOLD

THE ROUNDUP ~ TROUBLE BREWING, TROUBLE ON THE GROUND

19.

As usual, when a large herd is gathered, we heard the cattle before we saw them. The five of us were pushing one hundred and three head of cows, calves, and steers we'd gathered up along the way. It took me back to when I'd first seen the Front Range of the Rocky Mountains. I was on a horse back then too, pushing more than a thousand head of cattle from Texas toward Wyoming. My friend Yellowhorse and I were working for Charlie Goodnight in those days. I had to smile. More than twenty years later, here I was pushing cattle again.

As we approached Haystack Rock, rather than take the long way around, we chose to go over the back of a smallish butte. From the top of the rise we had a good view of the flats where the herd was being held. Below us there were hundreds of cattle milling about. These were all range cattle of mixed breed. Most of the cows had calves, some a few weeks old, others born more recently.

Over at the base of Haystack Rock, a cow camp had been set up. Some wagons had been pulled into a circle on the edge of a stand of piñon and scrub pine. In the center of the circle a mixed batch of tables and chairs had been assembled under a big tent cover. Between here and there, spread out around the edges of the herd, were about a dozen mounted men holding the cattle together on the flats. A small creek meandered through the middle of the herd.

As we started our bunch down the slope, a couple of riders peeled away from the larger herd and split up to help us ease our cattle into the bigger group. Once that was accomplished one of the riders trotted up beside me and Ace Johnson.

"Mornin' Mr. Johnson. Who's this feller?" The rider asked, looking me over.

"Mornin' Ed. Shake hands with John, here. He's repping for the Rocking M."

The man showed a sudden interest as he reached over and shook my offered hand.

233

"Ed Baxter, Mr...I didn't catch your last name." He said, giving me a sharp look.

"You can call me John. All my friends do."

"OK, John. I'm the foreman for the Bar C Bar. I heard someone was claiming to represent the Murphy outfit, but the story I heard was the Rocking M is abandoned."

"Nope. A couple of the owners shifted into town, but I represent them. The other owner is here in the area."

"Other owner? I thought Murphy was the sole proprietor."

"Nope. He had a partner."

"Who's the partner?" He asked, clearly surprised by the whole conversation.

"Now, that isn't really any of your business. Is it, Ed?"

His gaze wandered away toward the snow-capped peaks. Ed pulled his hat off and wiped the sweat band with his bandana. He pulled it back on and looked over at me.

"No. I reckon not. You might want to think about keeping that bit of information to yourself. My boss is a mighty nosey man. All he needs to know is you're riding for the Rocking M. Do you understand what I'm saying?"

Seeing this exchange, Ace spoke up.

"Where do you stand in all this, Ed? Seems to me you're a reasonable man."

Ed shook his head.

"There's trouble brewing. I want no part of it, but I ride for the brand." He looked at me again. "Same as you, John."

He turned his horse and trotted back to the edge of the herd.

"What do you make of that?" Ace asked.

"He's some worried. Ed knows he's thrown in with the wrong outfit, but he can't back up. Not that kind of man." I said.

He gave me a look.

"I expect you aint either."

"Nope. Got no backup in me. It drives my wife crazy."

"Then he was right. There will be trouble."

"I won't start it, but if it comes my way, I aim to finish it. What do you say we check out the camp and figure what to do next?"

"Sounds like a plan."

***

At the Johnson wagon, Ace's daughters had a cook fire going with coffee on, so we all climbed down to get a cup. I looked over the set up. Each ranch had their own little area for cooking and bedding down by their wagon. Most were just buckboards or freight wagons they used every day on the ranch. I wished there was a real chuckwagon like Charlie Goodnight had built. Still, the Johnsons had a chuckbox on their wagon, outfitted as a mobile pantry and field kitchen. Those girls sure knew how to use it.

The arrangement was each ranch had their own gear and cook fire, but come meal time we could go from one wagon to the other to visit and sample all the victuals. In the heat of the day or the event of rain, we'd all eat together under the tent canopy. The crews holding or working the cattle would rotate in and out.

Off to one side of the camp, the horses were all thrown into one remuda. There were about a dozen head being held inside a rope corral. Other than our mounts now picketed outside the wagons, the other horses were being ridden by the men holding the incoming cattle and the herd. A wagon loaded with hay was parked nearby. The older kids would be responsible for feeding and leading the horses out to water at the creek.

I liked the lay out.

There were a few men sitting at a table in the shade, so we left our horses with the boys and headed that way to palaver.

As we approached, one of the men called out.

"Howdy, Ace. I see you have most of your older kids here with you. How's the Missus?"

"She's fit as a fiddle and about as high strung, Kermit. How's Carol? I expect she's pretty busy with the little ones, huh?"

"Yep. She'll probably come on out when we're finishing up. Who's this you have with you?"

"My name's John. I ride for the Rocking M."

The men at the table all glanced around at each other.

"Welcome, John. I'm Kermit Wilson. I own the Flying W, just south of here." The first speaker said.

"Pleasure." I said. I looked around at the three other men who hadn't spoken up.

Their attention turned to a well-dressed man sitting at the end of the table. He wore a sombrero with a silver studded band. Beyond that he was dressed like a business man., right down to the celluloid collar and tie with a pearl stickpin. His grey wool suit pants were tucked into fancy custom boots with a −C− brand worked into the front of the uppers.

Grabbing the lapels of his vest, he tilted his head back and looked down his nose at me.

"The Rocking M is finished. I don't know who you think you are, but you have no business here."

I nodded.

"I can see how you might think that, but we just gathered and drove in over a hundred head of cattle. Of those, twenty three cows carry the Rocking M brand. They all have calves. There were another eleven head of Rocking M steers. I expect once the gather is done, there'll be at least three hundred head of Rocking M cattle on this range. Probably more than a dozen horses, too. I don't call that finished. Like I say, I'm repping for the Rocking M. Who are you to say different?"

The man's face turned beet red.

"I'm Jud Coltrane. I own the biggest ranch in these parts. I took over the Rocking M when it was abandoned. You say you brought in cattle wearing the Rocking M brand? Unless your name is Murphy, you need to ride away before we mistake you for a rustler!"

Four riders leading a packhorse were approaching in a cloud of dust. Everyone's attention turned to them. The four bearded men rode right up to the edge of the tent.

"Howdy, John, how the hell are you?" Curt Cross said. "Ace." He added, with a nod.

"Mornin', Curt, Carl, Ken. How are you, Calvin. Glad to see you boys could make it." I said.

Jud Coltrane and the other men with him observed the greeting with mixed expressions.

"How do you know each other?" Coltrane snapped.

"I told you, I ride for the Rocking M. I've visited with some of the other ranchers. I asked the Johnsons and the Cross brothers to throw in with me. We'll help each other sort and brand our stock. The Rocking M has a lot more cattle than I can handle alone. Seems like a good arrangement , don't you think?"

Coltrane just sat there, his face red, struggling to respond.

"Sure thing. We all help each other. It's the way we've always done it." Kermit Wilson said.

"No. You're not welcome here. You have no claim on the Rocking M. It looks to me like you and these men are just a bunch of rustlers who banded together to steal our cattle." Coltrane said.

"You talk too damned much, Coltrane. You shut the hell up, or I'll climb off this horse and cut your damned throat for you." Carl said, pulling his Bowie knife from his boot.

Jud Coltrane paled at that.

"Easy now, Jud. Maybe these fellas do ride for the Rocking M." Kermit Wilson said. "If Ace Johnson says their legit, that's good enough for me."

Jud Coltrane didn't say another word. He stood up and walked away from the table. Two of the other men looked at each other and silently left the table, hurrying to catch up with Coltrane.

20.

The Cross brothers rode off to set up camp.

"John I don't want those men hanging around my daughters." Ace said. "I've seen the way they look at em, especially Katie. If they start drinking…"

We'd returned to where his sons were holding our horses.

"Can't be avoided, Ace. As long as your girls are here cooking and looking after our camp, they'll be meeting and talking to every cowboy on the range. If it worries you, send them home. We'll make do."

"No, no. Most of the cowboys will treat the girls like the young ladies they are. When the roundup's over, I expect more'n one will be showing up at my place to court

Katie. But those Cross men are another story. I don't trust em."

"You don't trust them, or you don't trust your girls around them?"

Ace gave me a sharp look.

I laughed.

"Between the two of us and your sons, I reckon we can keep an eye on things. If it becomes a problem, we'll deal with it."

Ace nodded.

"I reckon so. It'll be an interesting experience for the girls. I just don't want no trouble comin' from it."

"You had to know bringing young ladies to a roundup would be cause for some excitement. One way or another, I figure we'll have all the trouble we can handle. Listen, I'm going to ride out and have another word with Coltrane's foreman. I want to learn what the plan is for tomorrow."

246

Ace shrugged.

"Should be the same way we always do. Tonight, after supper, there'll be a meeting of the ranchers or the men representing the ranches. We'll elect a range boss. He'll tell us how he wants us to divide up the work. We'll have a crew holding the herd, another crew to sort and separate the cows with calves. Some of the hands will do the roping. Others will do the branding and castrating. We generally start right after breakfast. Course we'll need riders to take turns on night hawk. By supper time tonight, near every critter on the range will be here."

"What do we do between now and then?"

"It's more important than ever that we get an accurate nose count of your beef. I should say, the Rocking M cattle. Tomorrow there'll be an official tally, but by supper time tonight, you need to know roughly how many head you have here. That way we can make a case against any funny counting tomorrow. I expect everybody's doin' the same."

"Makes good sense to me, I'll get started." I said.

"Hold on, John. Can I make a suggestion?"

"Sure, I don't have a clue what I'm doing, Ace. You know the way things work on this range."

Ace crossed his arms.

"Here's the thing. On this roundup, me, my boys, and the Cross brothers are riding for the Rocking M. That means we work for you."

"Well, the Cross brothers don't really ride for the Rocking M. They've just kind of thrown in with us. Besides, what am I supposed to do?"

RIDING FOR THE BRAND

"You're the head man for the Rocking M. That makes you the foreman, John. You tell us what to do. I reckon you should send us to do the nose count and spell some of them holding the herd. This afternoon if you want to ride herd, you can. If you want to hang around here and meet the other outfits as they come in, do that. You're the boss. It's up to you."

I thought it over. He was right and it was time I accepted the responsibility.

"OK. Here's what we'll do. As soon as lunch is ready, we'll eat. Then, you and the others should figure on riding out to spell some of the drovers on the herd, so they can come in and eat. I'll ride along so I can meet some of those men. We'll get a nose count while we're at it. Between now and then, send your boys out to tell those men we'll be taking over for them in an hour or so. I want you with me when I talk to the Cross brothers. I mean to do that, right now."

"That's a good plan." Ace said. He looked at his sons who were standing there watching us. "You heard the man. Mount up and get to work."

***

As we walked toward the Cross camp, I glanced at Ace.

"You said something about the other outfits coming in. We know the Flying W is represented. So is the Bar C Bar, the Rocking M, Rafter J, and the Box Cross. I didn't get to meet those two gentlemen who are following along in Coltrane's shadow. Who are they?"

"I don't know. I expect Kermit could tell us."

"What other outfits are missing?"

"It ain't that anybody's missing, exactly. I think the ranches are all represented. Most of the owners are here, but a lot of the cattle are still being rounded up. There'll be at least a couple hundred more head along with a bunch of horses coming in this afternoon, more cowboys, too."

I had a thought, so I changed direction.

"Where we going?" Ace asked.

"I want to have a look at the remuda. There may be some Rocking M horses in the bunch."

"Should be. We didn't see any in our gather, but most of the Bar C Bar riders are already here. Except for the foals and young stock, all of Murphy's horses were well broke. Not a bronc or jug head among um, and Murphy knew good horseflesh when he saw it. Those Bar C Bar waddies like Rocking M horses. I reckon Coltrane figures they're his now. If you hadn't shown up, I reckon he'd have changed the brands."

"How many head did Murphy have?"

"At last count, four cow ponies, six brood mares, four two year olds, and five foals. Those were the saddle stock. He also had two big Belgians. Those were the work horses."

"So, twenty one head. When was the last count?"

"The Spring roundup."

Looking over the remuda, two of the fourteen horses in the rope corral wore the Rocking M brand, including one brown horse with a bald face. I wondered if his name might be Shongaloo. Only two Rocking M saddle horses present in the remuda suggested the other two cow ponies were probably under saddle somewhere. Maybe holding the herd, the rest were missing.

252

"Do they hold the range horses with the cattle during the roundup?"

"Not the breeding stock. They'd leave them on the range or corral um at home. "

I gave that some thought as we walked over to the Cross camp.

When we reached the place in the trees where the Cross brothers had made their camp, we found all four of them standing together, talking. They gave us the stink eye as we walked up.

"Howdy, boys, I sure am glad you decided to join us." I said, offering my hand to shake.

"Howdy, your own self. Who says we're joining anybody?"

I was a little taken aback by their attitude.

"What John means is he was hoping you'd help us with the Rocking M herd. He'll have about three hundred head. Me and mine are helping him out. What do you say?"

"Hell no. We just come to make sure nobody slapped the wrong brand on any of our cattle. I reckon we have a hundred head ourselves." Curt said.

Ace chuckled.

"Now, Curt, you boys know you didn't have but about thirty head at the Spring roundup. Half of them were steers. Did you eat any of them? You may have another eight or ten calves on the ground now, so your count will be more like forty head, tops. Not a hundred."

"We ain't got much of a handle on numbers. We'll take what's ours. Aint nobody gonna stop us, neither."

I watched this exchange and figured I knew what the problem was.

"I'll tell you what. You help us with our herd and we'll help you with yours. I figure you should get something for your troubles. How bout I let you have half a dozen of the Rocking M calves?"

"How many's that?" Carl asked.

"Six, Carl. You can have three Rocking M heifers and three bull calves or steers. You put your brand on them and they're yours."

"They'd have to be weanlings. We ain't got time to play nurse maid to no calves." Curt said.

"Fair enough. Six weanlings, and you get to pick em."

Ken was working it out on his fingers, as Curt and the others watched him. After a moment he nodded. "Damn, that's a good deal." he said.

"You bet. So, will you throw in with us?" Ace asked.

The four Cross brothers looked back and forth. After a moment Curt spoke for all of them.

"I reckon so." he said.

"There's something else that'll sweeten the deal. You boys can come and eat at our fire." Ace said.

"We brung our own grub." Calvin said.

"That's fine. I just want you to know you're welcome to my daughter's cooking."

The bearded men's faces were transformed by the thought.

"They'll have lunch ready any time now, if you're interested. Just one thing, I'll expect you to mind your manners around my daughters."

The Cross brothers stiffened a bit.

I decided to redirect the conversation.

"Here's the thing, boys, Ace is worried some wild cowboy will take a notion to say or do something bad to one of those girls. I'd sure appreciate it if you boys would help Ace protect his daughters.

Ace understood my thinking.

"My oldest daughter Katie is only sixteen. The other two are younger. They haven't been away from their momma's apron strings much."

The four men regarded him with somewhat less offended looks.

"Why sure, Ace. We'll watch out for um. Only, we never did know much about manners and such." Curt said.

"Do the best you can, then. Thank you. Mostly just try not to cuss in front of um."

"Why hell, Ace, we wouldn't do nothin' like that." Curt said.

Ace and I looked at each other for a moment, trying not to laugh.

"One other thing, boys. John is the foreman of the Rocking M. We take our orders from him. What he says goes. That OK with you?"

The brothers looked at each other, then back at me.

"Maybe so, maybe not. We'll ride for the brand, but we ain't much for taking orders." Curt said.

I grinned.

"That's capital, simply capital! As for taking orders, we'll all work together. I don't intend to boss you around."

RIDING FOR THE BRAND

We shook hands on it.

DAN ARNOLD

21.

Lunch passed without incident. The girls served up cold ham sandwiches and hot potato soup.

The Cross brothers tended to stare at Ace's oldest daughter, Katie, a little more than might be considered proper, but she was shaping up to be a stunner. She just ignored their stares. Ace was watchful but otherwise seemed unconcerned.

We ate quickly, thanked the ladies and mounted up to tend the herd.

The Rocking M now boasted nine riders. This was an impressive number for the size of the ranch. Of course there were really three ranches represented, but in the ways that mattered we were one. The other ranches would see us as one outfit working the roundup. I was thankful to have these men with me. I was mindful that just a few days before, I'd ridden into this country all alone.

As we approached the edge of the herd, Ed Baxter trotted over to meet us.

"Here comes that bastard, Baxter," Curt Cross said. "Coltrane's lap dog."

"Easy, Curt, I'm none too fond of him myself, but we all need to get along. At least till the roundup's over." Ace said.

"Then what? I reckon he'll go back to tearin' down your fences." Ken Cross said

"There's been no trouble, lately. Let's keep it that way." I said quietly.

I called out to the Bar C Bar rider, as he reined in. "Howdy, Ed. we've come out to help hold the herd. You and your boys can go on in and grab something to eat

Ed Baxter looked us over. Evidently, seeing the nine of us in a group puzzled him.

"Appreciate that. You men all riding together?"

"Yep, we ride for the Rocking M. You got a problem with that?" Curt asked.

"No problem. Who's in charge?"

Ace glanced my way.

"I am." I said.

Ed Baxter rubbed his face with a gloved hand. It was evident he was not happy with the news.

"OK, John. Have your men spread out and relieve one rider at a time. It doesn't matter what outfit they're with. Just hold your part of the herd, keep em bunched, but don't rile em. They're pretty quiet now, but there'll be a few hundred head coming in. They'll need to be eased in with the rest. Can you handle it?"

"We've got it." I said.

"OK. We'll meet up after supper to pick the range boss. I expect I'll see you at supper time. By then, there'll be some other riders to hold the herd."

He raised a hand in farewell as he trotted off toward the camp.

"Well, boys, you heard the man. Spread out and relieve one man at a time. I'm going to hang back to meet the riders coming in. I'll be around if you need me." I said.

Without saying another word the Johnsons and the Cross brothers turned their horses and split up.

I rode a little way back toward the camp to a high spot where I could watch the herd and meet the riders coming in for lunch.

The third rider quitting the herd was mounted on a Rocking M horse. I'm in the habit of holding my reins in my left hand. He wasn't. I stopped him and introduced myself.

264

RIDING FOR THE BRAND

"Howdy. My name's John. I'm the foreman for the Rocking M. You're sitting on one of our mounts. When you get to the camp, I'd sure appreciate it if you'd unsaddle him and turn him out in the remuda. You can pick a Bar C Bar horse to ride."

"I don't believe I will. I don't take orders from strangers. Who the hell do you think you are?"

I swung Dusty in front of him.

"It doesn't matter who I am. I asked you kindly. You seem to be on the prod. If you want to make a fight, do it now."

He was thinking about it, but he was holding his reins in his right hand, his gun hand. When he started to change hands on the reins, I leveled my Colt at him. He was smart enough to freeze.

"What's it going to be?" I asked.

"Mister, you swing a mighty wide loop. You don't know what a shit storm you just started. When I come back out here, I'll still be on this horse and I'll have more men with me. Then we'll see what's what."

"Nope. You won't be on that horse, because you're going to step off him, right now." I cocked the Colt. I didn't intend to shoot him, mostly because he was unarmed and he wouldn't have a chance, even if he reached for his gun. Also, gunfire might spook the herd. But looking into the barrel of my Colt, he didn't know my thoughts.

He looked a little pale, knowing he couldn't win. He stepped down, taking care not to let his hand get near his gun.

"That's good. Now drop the reins. While you're dropping things, pull that pistol and drop it in the saddle bag there. Easy now, I'd hate to shoot you by accident."

266

The man did as directed.

"Ok, start walking. I'll follow along just to make sure you make it back safely."

As he set off on foot, I eased Dusty up next to the Rocking M horse, scooped up the reins and followed the man back toward the camp. I almost felt sorry for him. A cowboy hates to be set afoot and this fellow would be walking into camp in disgrace.

I was worried about what kind of reception we'd get at the camp site, so I decided to try avoiding the drama.

"Hold up for a minute. I want a word with you."

He stopped walking and turned around to look at me.

"What's your name?" I asked.

"Gabe Partridge"

"You ride for the Bar C Bar?"

"Yep."

Well, Mr. Partridge, I ran into a couple of other Bar C Bar cowboys, riding Rocking M horses, a few days ago. I told them I wanted to see a bill of sale. Did you hear about that?"

"Yep."

"I'm not trying to pick a fight. This horse is a Rocking M mount. You don't own it and neither does your boss. We're going to need all our horses to work the roundup. I told you, I'm the foreman for the Rocking M. What would you do if you were me?"

He squinted for a moment and scuffed the ground with his right boot. He considered giving me a wise crack answer, but thought better of it.

"I reckon I'd do the same as you."

"Well then, I'll ask again, Gabe. Will you please take this horse and turn it out in the remuda? Put your tack on a Bar C Bar

268

horse and we'll be square. I've got no gripe with you."

It only took him a moment to make up his mind.

"I reckon so."

"I sure appreciate it. Here, take this horse to the remuda, then go get you some lunch." I handed him the reins. "I expect I'll see you around."

He nodded a silent answer.

I turned Dusty and trotted back the way we'd come.

DAN ARNOLD

22.

As the afternoon stretched out, other riders brought in large and small bunches of cattle. The herd now swelled to more than a thousand head. Some of the cowboys from the other ranches pitched in to help hold the herd while others went on to the camp site.

As supper time approached, I rode around to each of our men to get an idea of who wanted to stay with the herd and who wanted to go back to camp.

"I'll ride in with you, if that's OK? My boys can stay with the herd and eat later. I need to check on the girls and I want to be at the meeting after supper." Ace said.

"Sure, Ace. I should go find the Cross brothers and ask them what they want to do."

"You're the boss. You tell them what you want."

"I want them with us in camp."

"Well then let's go fetch um. I'm ready to eat a thing."

***

A short while later as we turned our horses in with the remuda, we noticed two things; the light hearted atmosphere in the camp and the smell of piñon smoke, mixed with the savory odors of multiple meals prepared over the coals of the cook fires. Men were eating at the tables under the canopy, laughing and cutting up. Several cowboys were lined up to get food from the Rafter J cook fire. By the way they were sweeping their hats off and generally acting gallant; it was pretty obvious the food wasn't the biggest attraction.

"Looks like we'll need to bust a few damned heads." Calvin Cross said.

"Easy does it boys. There's no problem here. It's only natural. Bees are drawn to flowers and those girls are as pretty as daisies. Besides, they could cook a skunk and make it taste like doughnuts and honey. Those fellas are doing their best to be charming and princely."

"I reckon, but if one of them damned waddies gets out of line, I'll fetch him, for sure." Carl Cross said.

Everybody in camp watched us walk in. The friendly banter stopped for a moment, then resumed anew.

A sandy haired young man, with a freckled face, grinned as we approached. He looked to be about twenty and he was all cowboy.

"Hey, Mr. Johnson. I reckon this is the best grub at the roundup. I don't understand how you stay trim. You should be fat as a prize hog. Do you always eat like this at your place?"

"Howdy, Buster. Sure do. I stay fit by working my backside off. You might want to give it a try."

"Naw, not me. I was born lazy and I'm too stupid to change."

Everybody laughed, including Buster.

Katie was shyly looking at Buster with some curiosity.

Since this was our cook fire, we got our plates and the girls loaded us up, as the other cowboys waited for whatever was left over. They didn't mind waiting, it gave them some time to admire the girls, under the watchful glare of Ace and the four Cross brothers.

Ace looked over the growing knot of riders assembling around us. He shook his head and spoke up.

"Say now, there's not much left but gristle and gravy. My sons will need to eat what's here. I reckon some of you boys will have to fetch your grub from your own cook fires."

The assembled men looked abashed, then grinned at each other. A couple of them nodded and turned away. After that, most of the others drifted away, too. Buster stayed though, relaxed and casual, like he was used to standing while he ate. He was hovering around Katie.

"Buster, go get us some seats at the table." Ace said.

After saying thank you to the girls, Buster did as he'd been told.

"That boy seems mighty interested in Katie. Who is he?"

"...Buford Cavender. He's about the best young bronc fighter and all around horseman in these parts. That's why everybody calls him 'Buster'. He breaks horses for everybody and anybody...goes from ranch to ranch."

"He seems like a decent sort."

"Umm hmm. All kidding aside, that boy is one of the hardest working young men I ever saw. Hell of a hand."

As we found our seats, there were various nods and casual greetings all around.

I scanned the crowd. I saw a couple of familiar faces. Coltrane wasn't among them. I found a seat next to Kermit Wilson, the owner of the Flying W.

"Mr. Wilson, I was hoping you could tell me who those men were that left with Mr. Coltrane, earlier.

"…Cattle buyers from Denver. You can call me Kermit, John."

"Thanks. Why would somebody from Denver come here to buy cattle?"

"Denver's growing fast. The demand for beef is causing prices to go up. They don't want to pay to have cattle shipped in from Texas or wherever. Local stock is plentiful, available and priced right. They could buy several hundred head here, and have them driven down to Denver in two days. They have a packing plant down there. It was Jud's idea to invite em. I reckon it's a good deal for everybody."

I nodded. It really was a good idea. If the price was right, it would benefit the cattle brokers who could sell beef in Denver, all winter, without having to have any shipped in. The local ranchers would have some ready cash, no shipping charges and less cattle to feed through the winter.

"Jud can probably sell a couple hundred head of steers and a couple dozen culls, old cows poor calves and what not. If what you say about having three hundred head is true, the Rocking M probably has at least a hundred head you could sell."

"Our estimated nose count today came to about three hundred and twelve."

"There you go. I'm told the Flying W has about two hundred head. That's comes to about a thousand head between just our three ranches. The rest are in smaller bunches. The buyers could probably have nearly five hundred head, if they want that many."

"I expect Coltrane is handling the deal, right?"

Kermit gave me a sharp look'

"Sure. He made the arrangements and he's wining and dining the buyers at his own expense. Do you have a problem with that?"

"Can you trust him?"

Kermit seemed irritated. He made a face confirming it

"You think he's making a little extra on the side? So what if he is? He's done the work to set up the deal. I'm OK with that, how about you?"

"Have you asked the other ranchers how they feel about it?"

Kermit stood up. He leaned over and spoke quietly but firmly to me.

"If you don't like the offer, you don't have to sell. Nobody does." He looked around at the men within ear shot. "Listen up, everybody! We'll meet right here in thirty minutes. We need to choose a range boss and make plans for tomorrow. Thirty minutes. That's all." He turned and walked away.

I felt bad about annoying Kermit. I needed to make friends, not enemies. What he hadn't considered was, before I showed up, Coltrane had been planning to sell Rocking M cattle. He might've sold off the whole herd, at one hundred percent pure profit. Now that I was here, representing the Rocking M, it had cost Coltrane a few thousand dollars and would cause untold trouble. He wasn't the kind of man to let anything slide. He'd been crossed and he would do something about it. Kermit Wilson didn't know my riding for the brand had lit the fuse to a powder keg.

I couldn't see the Cross brothers anywhere at the table. When I walked back to the wagon, I found Curt Cross sitting on a bucket watching the girls doing the cleanup chores.

"Where are your brothers?"

"We drew straws to see who'd look out for the girls, till their brothers come in, and I lost. It ain't too bad though."

It dawned on me the Cross brothers hadn't had a drink all day.

"Are they over at your camp?"

"I reckon."

"Thanks, Curt. I'll head over there."

"I'll be along directly, myself. Save me a swig." He winked.

***

I found the Cross brothers sitting around their fire, passing a bottle.

"Hello the camp, can I come in?"

"Hell yes, if'n you brought your own booze." Carl sneered.

"Nope, I think I've taken the cure. I just wanted to know if y'all are going to come to the meeting."

"We ain't much for meetings. This here's our meeting, but you're welcome to join us."

"They're going to divvy up the chores. I just need to know what you boys want to do. If you're good at roping, sorting, branding or whatever, What do you do best?"

The bearded men looked around at each other. Ken spoke up.

"We're good at making shine." He belched. They all laughed.

"I know that's right. Seriously though, we've got a job of work to do over the next couple of days. Where do you want me to put you?"

Carl winked at his brothers." I reckon the branding fire is good. We're good with the irons."

His comment suggested they had some experience altering brands with a running

iron, a common practice among rustlers. I
didn't much like what he was suggesting, but
it wasn't my problem. Besides, maybe it was
just the whisky talking.

"Figure on it then. We'll get started at
first light. We'll need at least three fires-one
for each of the bigger outfits. Some of the
cowboys will rope the calves and mavericks
and drag em to the edge, where you'll slap
iron to em, and somebody will cut the bull
calves."

"Damn. I'm sure looking forward to
them oysters." Ken said.

"Oysters?"

"Ken looked at me like I was crazy.
"What, you never et no Rocky Mountain
oysters?"

"Oh, sure, I get it. In Texas we called
em calf fries."

"Call em what you like, bull calves nuts is some damned good eating. Who'll do the cutting?"

"I don't have any idea. Somebody who's good at, I expect. We can't afford any greenhorn mistakes."

"Yep, like accidently slapping the wrong brand on a critter." They all laughed at that idea, as though it were a private joke.

"Whoever ropes the calf will bring it to the right fire, and tell you what outfit it belongs to."

"And we're just supposed to trust em?"

I shrugged.

"We're all working together on this. Each outfit is represented. We each have a tally, and the range boss will work to see everything gets done fairly. It shouldn't be a problem."

"Won't be a problem, so long as we get all our stock counted right." Calvin Cross said.

I could tell the liquor was having its intended effect. He was moody and slurring his words.

"I'll make sure of it. If there's a problem, you can take it up with me. I'll see you boys at first light."

I took the opportunity to walk away before the conversation turned ugly.

DAN ARNOLD

23.

The assembled cowboys chose Ed Baxter as the range boss. It came as no surprise. All the locals knew him and he'd proven his ability in previous roundups, earning the trust of every man in attendance— except me. Still, I had no objection and I couldn't think of anyone better qualified.

He first assigned the skilled jobs to men who had proven ability.

"Buster, you're the wrangler in charge of the remuda. Hank, I reckon you, Luke, Jeff and Dennis are the best ropers among us. You boys'll be busy. I'm told the branding will be handled by the Cross brothers. That's fine with me. Anybody got an objection? Ace, you, Scott, and Glen will do the castrating. Justin, you have a fine cuttin' horse. Pick two or three fellas with good horses to help you sort and move mamma cows and calves to where the ropers can do their work. John, I want you to help me manage the count. Right now, I need volunteers for nighthawks."

Several cowboys raised their hands, including all three of Ace's sons. Ace didn't like it. I could tell by his frown when they volunteered, but he couldn't interfere. It left just him and me to watch the girls at night.

"The rest of you will hold the herd and pitch in as needed. I want the youngsters to stay clear of the action. You older boys can help keep the branding fires hot, otherwise— stay out of the way. This work ain't easy and it's dangerous. If we all pitch in and stay alert, we won't have any trouble we can't handle. Any questions? No? Alright, that's it then. We start at first light."

As the meeting broke up I found Ed Baxter and asked if I could have a private word with him.

"…Something on your mind, John?"

"I was just surprised you asked me to help you with the tally."

"Why, you can count, can't you?"

"Sure, I just figured…"

"Everybody gets a fair count. Everybody. Do you have a problem with that?"

"Of course not."

"Here, take this notebook and pencil. Write the name of the ranch or brand. Make a mark for every cow or steer we count with a particular brand. Do the same for the calves as they get branded. We'll tally it all up at the end and compare notes. We should be pretty close—if not exactly the same."

"Fair enough. I just wanted to say thanks for including me."

""We all do what we can. You do your job and I'll do mine." He turned and walked off into the night.

I scratched at my chin, feeling the beard stubble. Ed Baxter was as unknown and unpredictable as a wild range bull. He seemed honest and fair, but he worked for a man who was just the opposite. Where would Ed Baxter stand, when it came down to it?

***

Back at the cook fire, I discovered Ace and the girls had rolled out my bedroll, next to Ace's, under the wagon. The girls had their bedrolls made up in the wagon under the cover of the tarp. It afforded them some privacy and if it rained we should all stay reasonably dry.

Ace and Buster were sitting by the fire with the girls, drinking coffee.

"You girls go on to bed, now. Dawn comes mighty early and we'll want hot coffee with bacon and biscuits before we get to work. Give me a kiss and say good night to these gentlemen." Ace said.

I couldn't help noticing Buster and Katie had been showing signs of mutual attraction, smiling and exchanging glances and the occasional brief words. If Ace saw it, he made no comment.

As soon as the girls left us, I decided to mention the pending conflict with the horses.

"Buster, including my buckskin, the Rocking M has five horses in the remuda. The thing is; Bar C Bar cowboys rode four of them here. It seems Jud Coltrane figured on adding them to his cavvy. I expect to use our own stock without any interference from the Bar C Bar crowd. You being the wrangler, it might put you in a pickle. How do you want to handle it?"

In the warm light of the campfire the young man looked thoughtful for a moment.

"It won't be a problem. I'm the wrangler. I tend the herd, doctor injuries, and make sure none of the horses gets overused. I assign horses as I see fit. If a horse carries a Rocking M brand, it goes to a Rocking M rider. I'll see to it. End of story."

"I hope it goes that smoothly."

"Like I say, I'm the wrangler. It's my saddle on this bronc, it's mine to ride. I figure I'll get it done. You folks have a good night. I'm gonna make sure none of the nighthawks gets the wrong mount. See you in the morning."

Sipping his coffee, Ace watched this exchange without expression. When Buster was out of earshot, I turned to ask him a question.

"What do you think?"

Ace shrugged and stood up, brushing the dust off his clothes.

"I reckon I'm ready to get some shut eye,"

"Do you think Buster can handle it?"

Ace stared into the fire for a moment, a crooked smile forming on his face.

"I expect so. That boy has sand."

DAN ARNOLD

24.

Morning found us up and getting organized while the stars were still bright in the sky. I awakened feeling oddly refreshed and, though a bit stiff, well rested. There's something about being exhausted that makes sleeping on the ground under a wagon downright enjoyable. I realized I hadn't had a nightmare since I rode into this Buttercup country. I thanked God for that. I was missing Lora and the children something awful, but took comfort knowing I was doing what needed to be done.

As the eastern horizon started to grow lighter, the girls had hot coffee and victuals ready for us. It was especially nice, since there was a significant chill to the early morning air.

"Frosty this mornin'." Ace said. "Glad we've about got all our hay put up. Be winter before you know it and there's too many cattle on this range. It's time to cull and sell off some of the stock."

"You aren't the only one thinking it. It just so happens, Jud Coltrane has a plan. Those two men who left with him are cattle buyers from Denver. He's already made some sort of deal with them." I said.

"Good. He's the reason there's too many cattle anyways. I reckon he's smart enough to see that."

"He's smart, but he figured on selling off the Rocking M herd. His profit margin went up in smoke when I showed up."

Ace gave me a concerned look and said, "That's some serious money. He's not a man who likes to be crossed. You'd better watch your back."

I didn't answer, because right then the Cross brothers showed up for breakfast. They were a pretty bedraggled looking bunch, but no worse than usual. They grunted in reply or ignored our early morning greetings, grabbing plates and loading up without so much as a thank you to the girls. They snatched up one of the coffee pots for their own personal use.

Right behind them, the boys who'd been riding nighthawk dragged in. They were clearly tired, but also held themselves with the kind of dignity that comes with having done a grown man's work and done it well.

I saw some pride on Ace's face as he greeted them.

"I reckon you boys'll want to catch some shut eye, but we'll need all hands if we want to get everything done today. You can sleep tonight."

"Hey, Pa, is there gonna be a party tonight?" Jimmy Johnson asked.

"Not exactly, but if the weather holds, the women folk will come on out. We'll have some music and what not."

"So, we'll be done this evening?" I asked.

"…Maybe before suppertime. There's three or four hundred head to be branded and cut. Three branding fires slapping brands on three critters every few minutes, that'll be fifty or sixty head per hour, between the three fires." Ace said.

"That's fast work, and some fancy calculating on your part."

"Yep, and it includes cutting the bull calves and trading out tired horses. Won't be no time for lolly gaggin' or day dreamin', though." He directed that last comment at his

298

boys. All three of them looked like they were ready to fall asleep on their feet.

"What happens to the herd after all the work is done?"

"Usually, we just let em go. Might be different this time on account of sortin' out the cattle we're gonna sell."

"I'll want to cut the Rocking M stock out of the bigger herd." I said.

"Shouldn't be a problem. We're sorting and gathering a bunch for sale anyways. Work out the details with the range boss."

***

I found Ed Baxter outside the makeshift horse pen. Buster was pointing out horses to riders from the various outfits, who would then throw a loop over the head of their first mount for the morning.

My conversation with the range boss was much easier than I'd expected. He listened to my plans and nodded.

"That's fine. I'm figuring on holding the herd overnight. At the stockyard in Buttercup, there's good pens that'll hold three hundred head or more. Tomorrow morning, we'll all pitch in to sort out the cattle we're gonna sell, and then my outfit will drive the sale stock over to the holding pens. If you're planning to separate your herd from the rest, that'll be a good time to do it. Everybody will help you sort and gather your herd, and then you and your crew can drive them on to the Rocking M." Ed Baxter said.

I was surprised he was so agreeable.

"Are you sure it's not a problem? Your boss seems to think I've got no claim to the Rocking M stock."

"That's between you and him. I'm the range boss. I make the decisions about how we handle the roundup. That includes how the stock gets sorted."

"He might not see it that way."

"Then that'll be between him and me."

"I figured you wouldn't want to get crossways with him."

"I don't and I won't. Mr. Coltrane can tell me what he wants me to do with the Bar C Bar cattle, and I'll do it. He doesn't get to tell me what to do with the roundup."

It seemed to me Ed Baxter was riding a mighty narrow and dangerous trail. I figured from his perspective it was the only way to manage the situation.

"Alright, it's fine by me. I appreciate the help." I said.

"It's how we always do. It's the same for everybody."

"OK, thanks." I said, starting to turn away.

"Just one thing, though."

I turned back to face him.

"What's that?"

"When the roundup's over, I ride for the Bar C Bar."

"And your point is…?"

"I do what Mr. Coltrane tells me. I expect he's got plans for you. You know what I'm saying?"

I met his gaze.

"Like you said, that's between him and me."

"Just so you know. I ride for the brand."

"Then, just so you know. When the roundup's over, I've got plans of my own for him. You don't want to get between us."

"Don't want to, but it might go that way."

"It's a free country. You do what you have to. I'll do the same."

"I reckon so." He said, "Just so you know."

DAN ARNOLD

25.

I hadn't seen Jud Coltrane since the first meeting at the start of the roundup. I hadn't seen Snake or his big ugly partner either. It had me guessing. Why were they staying away from the roundup? Were they just waiting to catch me alone at the Rocking M? That would be the way Coltrane would want to do it. He liked to have other men do his fighting for him, and he was patient enough to wait till the circumstances favored him.

I was too busy to worry about it. The morning flew by. I'd counted four hundred and ninety eight head by eleven o'clock. Two hundred and seventeen of those were calves, roped and dragged away from their mamas, to be branded and returned. More than half of

305

those were bull calves to be castrated at the branding fire. Many of the cattle to be sold now sported a big blob of white paint. That would make sorting them out much easier the next day. Things were going as smoothly as could be hoped.

When I'd stepped into the rope corral to get a horse, Buster told me my horse Dusty was too tired and a little bit saddle sore. He needed to rest up. Buster pointed to the brown horse with the white face and a Rocking M brand. I stepped up to him with my rope in hand and eased a loop over his head. He didn't even flinch.

"Hello, Shangaloo," I said. "You ready to go home to the Rocking M?"

The horse didn't answer, but he seemed agreeable. In short order we came to be friends. He impressed me as being wholly reliable and very well broke. I'd been on him for about five hours, when Ed Baxter rode over and asked me what my count was.

I checked my figures in the notebook he'd given me.

"I show four hundred and ninety eight head, so far. Two hundred and seventy one Bar C Bar, one hundred and thirty two Rocking M, sixty seven Flying W, seventeen Corkscrew and 10 Box cross. What do you reckon?"

The range boss looked at his notebook, his lips moving as he counted silently. He looked up and nodded.

"I reckon that's right. We're making good time, too. "

"That calf over there is still bleeding."

"Not much we can do about it. If we lose him, we lose him."

"He's one of your steers, freshly branded."

307

"Yep, we may all lose one or two before it's over. Broken necks, legs or what not, goes with the territory. I hope we get finished before the storm hits."

Clouds had been building and it was getting dark to the west, the mountains now hidden in the gathering gloom.

"I don't think so. It looks like it'll be here in an hour or so."

Ed studied the signs for a moment, listening to the distant thunder.

"I expect you're right, let's take a quick lunch break. I want everyone mounted and ready to help hold the herd when the storm hits. If there aint too much lightning, we'll be alright. We shouldn't lose much time in the rain. I remember one spring it rained so hard it put out the branding fires. Let's spread the word and get ready."

***

RIDING FOR THE BRAND

When the storm did hit, it came with crackling lightening, strong howling winds and a wall of cold rain. The first of it was the worst of it. The herd became agitated and would have scattered if we weren't all there to hold it. This was another example of why Ed Baxter was a good choice for range boss. He knew what needed to be done and made it happen. After about fifteen minutes, the lightening moved on and it settled into a steady rain.

"Alright, let's get back to work. I sure hope those boys were feeding the fires." Ed said.

It turned out they'd done their job. The branding fires were plenty hot. Within thirty minutes of the storm hitting, we were back in the rhythm of sorting, roping and branding. Although the muddy conditions made the work harder and more dangerous for

309

both the horses and the men on the ground, the rain barely slowed us.

The storm ended a couple of hours later. As the sun broke through the clouds, we were treated to a double rainbow.

A sudden commotion on the far side, near the middle of the herd, drew everyone's attention for a moment. I figured one of the sorters was having some problem with a mama cow or something. Some cows can be dangerously protective of their calves. Sometimes they have to be roped by two men so the calf can be roped and taken to the branding fires.

As a freshly branded calf scrambled up and ran back to his mama, I marked two more Rocking M cattle in the book.

A rider galloped toward us from the herd. As he slid to a stop, he called for Ace, who had just finished cutting a bull calf.

"What's wrong, Gabe?" He asked, wiping his bloody hands on the calf's flank.

"It's Jimmy, Mr. Johnson. Here, take my horse. You'd better hurry."

Ace took the reins from the rider's outstretched hand and leaped into the saddle. As he galloped away from the branding fire, I fell in beside him on Shangaloo, looking toward the herd for the cause of the emergency.

On the other side of the herd a knot of riders was assembling, others were moving cattle away from the spot. We neared the edge of the herd, slowing to work our way through without creating any more disturbance than necessary.

We pulled up where the knot of mounted men sat with bowed heads.

"Oh God, Jimmy!" Ace cried, jumping off the horse.

Jimmy Johnsons's broken and sodden body lay trampled into the mud and manure. Two men knelt beside him. One of the men was Ed Baxter. With his bandana, He was wiping the bloody mess away from Jimmy's now ash-white freckled face. The other man was Jimmy's older brother Henry.

"What happened here?" Ace moaned. He sat down in the filthy muck, pulling the boy's lifeless body into his arms.

"He was half asleep, Pa, not paying attention to where he was or what he was doing. He was hazing some bunch quitters back in and rode up behind a range bull and smacked him with his rope. I yelled to warn him, but it was too late. That bull spun around and hit Jimmy's horse like a freight train, knocked both of them over. His horse got away. Jimmy didn't. By the time I got here, it was too late. I was too late." Henry broke down, sobs wracking his body as he pounded his fists against his thighs.

The assembled cowboys watched in silence.

DAN ARNOLD

26.

Standing, Ed Baxter looked around at the men on horseback. He took off his hat and slapped it against his leg, shaking his head. He turned back to where Ace sat in the reeking muck cradling his son's mutilated body.

"Ace, you and your kids need to take Jimmy home. We'll help the girls get packed up. You can put his body in your wagon and take him home for burial. We'll finish up the day's work."

"No. It's OK. He's resting now. His mother will be along shortly. She was planning to come out for the end of the roundup, anyway. She and the girls can take him home and get him cleaned up. We'll bury him tomorrow, when the work is done."

"Ace, I'm so sorry about this. Please, take him home. Y'all need to be together." I said.

"There's work to be done. We didn't sign on to run home at the first sign of trouble.

You'll be short-handed as it is. Henry, ride out to find your mother. Bring her and the buckboard straight here. Where's Thomas?"

"Here, sir." Thomas Johnson had just ridden up and was standing directly behind Ace, holding his horse's bridle reins. He put his hand on his dad's shoulder.

Ace nodded.

"Thomas, go tell the girls what's happened. Help them get packed up, and then drive them back to the ranch. I'll see you tomorrow."

"Yes sir." Thomas Johnson stood staring at his father where he sat in the mud with his dead son in his lap. Thomas looked up at the sky, closing his eyes for a moment, and then he squared his young shoulders, looked at his brother Henry—who nodded, then they both mounted and rode away to complete their assignments.

"Some of you boys go with Thomas. Lend a hand. We'll stay with Ace till Mrs. Johnson gets here. The rest of you, get back to work. There're a couple of dozen more calves to brand and cut. Get it done." Ed said.

Two mounted men stayed to help me move the edge of the herd farther away from the men on the ground. I left them to hold the line and rode back to where Ed Baxter was talking to Ace, who was still sitting in the mud, holding Jimmy.

317

"It's my fault, you know? I pushed him too hard. I always do. I expect too much." Ace was saying.

"No, Ace. Those boys love and admire you. They want to be just like you. You've raised fine sons. This was an accident that could've happened to any of us." I said.

"I shouldn't have let him ride nighthawk. Maybe if he'd had some sleep…"

"Stop right there, Ace. Jimmy was doing a man's work. He wanted to do it and he did it well. It's not your fault. I'm the range boss. I asked for volunteers. I knew he was the youngest. I could've told him no. I didn't. This is something I have to live with. I hoped no one would get hurt, but this is dangerous work. I'm responsible for everyone and everything that happens on this roundup. If you want to blame someone, blame me." Ed said.

After a moment Ace sighed and shook his head.

"No, it's a hell of a thing, but it's what happens when we get careless. You're right, John. This could've been any of us. It only takes one mistake. Sometimes you don't get a second chance. I just don't know what I'm going to tell his mother."

I hadn't been completely honest with Ace. I blamed myself. Ace didn't have a single cow on this range, but I'd drafted him and his sons to help me. Now, one of his sons was dead. How could I tell him that? Well, if I couldn't tell Ace, I could and would tell his wife.

***

As the afternoon moved toward evening, we saw various wagons and people on horseback moving toward the campsite, then a buckboard with a lone rider alongside turned down a hillside directly toward the herd.

Ed had gone back to see to the last of the work, leaving me with Ace who still sat with Jimmy's body in his lap.

"Help me up, John. I don't want her to see me like this. I'm too stiff to get up by myself."

"Too late, she's here."

Mrs. Johnson stopped the buckboard directly in front of us. I hurried to help her down.

"Oh, Horace, our sweet, sweet boy, Jimmy." She said as she knelt beside Ace.

Ace couldn't speak. He just shook his head, looking down at Jimmy.

"Are you alright? Are you hurt?" She asked, taking Ace's face in her hands.

"No, I'm OK."

"Well then, let's put him in the buckboard."

I helped Ace get to his feet. It wasn't easy. He was nearly unable to stand.

"You're all stove up. What happened?" Mrs. Johnson asked him.

"Hard work, I've been bent over cutting bull calves all day and I sat here too long. I'll be alright in a minute." He said, stretching out the kinks. "Here, John, you and Henry help me with Jimmy?"

We put the mangled, muddied and now stone cold body of Jimmy Johnson in the back of the buckboard. Mrs. Johnson gently covered him with a blanket, tucking the blanket around her son one last time.

"Mrs. Johnson, I'm John Everett Sage. I want you to know how sorry I am about this. Your son is dead because of me. If I hadn't asked Ace for help, none of this would've happened."

"Oh really, Mr. Sage, are you God? I don't think so. The Lord gives and takes away. Blessed be the name of the Lord. He alone knows what a day may bring forth. Jimmy died doing what he loved to do. He was young and strong and handsome, just coming into his prime. He was a gift from God, who called him home. I'm proud to have known him and been his mother. You don't get to take that away from me, Mr. Sage."

"No, ma'am."

"Now, you men get on with your chores. You too, Henry, stay and help your father finish up. I'll see our Jimmy gets home and cleaned up. I met Thomas and the girls on the trail. Thomas and the other boys will build his coffin. We'll bury him when you all get home, tomorrow."

"We're moving the Rocking M herd onto the Murphy place first thing in the morning. It'll take a few hours, but we'll be home right after that." Ace told her.

"That's alright. It'll give us time to dig the grave. It's such rocky ground." She said.

I helped her up into the driver's seat.

She made eye contact with Ace, holding his hand for a moment and then without another word she slapped the lines and the chestnut horse trotted away.

The three of us stood watching as the buckboard disappeared over the top of the hill.

DAN ARNOLD

27.

We were a somber group pushing the Rocking M herd to the Murphy ranch. After we helped the Cross brothers cut their thirty six head out of the bigger herd, they'd turned for home.

I'd decided to sell one hundred head, including most of the mature steers and some culls. Those cattle were now part of more than four hundred being driven to the stock pens at Buttercup. That left us two hundred and eighteen to drive back to the ranch, mostly mama cows and calves. Several of the other hands helped us sort our cattle and get them on the trail. Then, once we were moving along smoothly, one by one, they peeled off to go home. That left just me, Ace, and his son Henry, to make the drive.

Because the three of us were efficient and the cattle were cooperative, at first the shortage of help wasn't too big of a problem. After a couple of miles we were having trouble holding them together and moving forward. We were saved because Thomas, Fred, Terry and Toby Johnson rode out to meet us. Everything went more smoothly after that.

As we approached the new fence boundary of the Rocking M, one of the boys opened the gate and we pushed the herd through the gap and onto the ranch. The gate was made of roughhewn lumber, swinging from a tall post on one side of the gap, suspended about a foot off the ground and balanced by a length of chain attached high on the post. The latch was just a loop of wire that was laid over the shorter post on the other side of the gap. Simple, but workman like.

When the gate was closed behind the cattle, we sat our horses for a moment, watching them spread out.

"Ace, I don't have words to thank you for all you've done. I'm much obliged. I'd like to come over to your place, once I get cleaned up. Could I be there when ya'll bury Jimmy? I'd be proud to say something."

"Yes. I expect he'd like that. As for being obliged, don't thank me. I did this in remembrance of Sean Murphy. I was obliged to him. He helped save the Rafter J and I let his children down."

"Still, I couldn't have done any of this without your help and...I'll be along in an hour or so."

"Better make it closer to noonday. Give us all time to get cleaned up. I don't know what has yet to be done."

"Nothing, Pa. We have Jimmy laid out in a pine box. He's wearing his Sunday go to meetin' clothes and everything."

Ace squeezed Thomas' shoulder, a sign of both appreciation and affection.

"What about the grave?" Henry asked.

"We dug it last night. We finished this fence yesterday evening. When we come in and found Ma with Jimmy…Anyway, we dug the grave last night." Toby said.

Ace blinked and looked away, nodding. He looked ten years older than he'd been the day we set off for the roundup.

"I'll come over around noon." I said.

Turning his horse toward home, Ace raised a hand in farewell, his boys falling in around him.

I opened the gate without having to step off Dusty, eased through and closed it. I sat for a moment looking over the cattle and the land. This was a good place. Good land, good water and the promise of a future for Jake and Sarah. I couldn't wait to tell Lora all about it.

I had some things to do between then and now.

***

I'd arranged to have Buster bring the Rocking M horses to the ranch. He'd be along any time now. I cleared it with Ed Baxter the day before when we finalized the count.

"Ed, there're four Rocking M mounts in the remuda. I intend to take them back to the ranch. Do you have a problem with that?"

"Course not, why should I?"

"Your boss seems to think they belong to him."

"Again, that's between you and him. Do you see him around here?"

329

"No, I don't. Why do you suppose that is?"

"He'll be along. We'll have the usual after roundup get together and whoop-ti-do in an hour or so. Losing Jimmy will kind of put a damper on things, but it's how we do at the end of a roundup. If those horses carry the Rocking M brand, as far as I'm concerned they can go with you."

"I'll ask Buster to bring them to the ranch. The young stock is missing, along with the work horses, wagons and other equipment from the Rocking M. I'll be coming out to the Bar C Bar to get what's been stolen."

Ed gave me a sharp look.

"Don't be a damned fool. I can't help you."

"I'm not asking for help. I'm just telling you how it's going to be. It's how I do."

He regarded me for a moment,

"Suit yourself. It's your funeral. One man is dead already, aint that enough?"

"Are you referring to Jimmy Johnson or Sean Murphy? Jimmy's death today was an accident. Sean Murphy was murdered. Your boss will answer for that. So will whoever helped him do it. Were you there when Murphy was lynched?"

"No. As the foreman, hanging rustlers goes with the job. I ride for the brand, but I was in Bear Creek when it happened."

"Do you believe Sean Murphy was a rustler?"

Ed Baxter looked away.

"No, no I never believed that."

"Might be why Coltrane waited till you were away from the ranch, don't you think?"

He shrugged.

331

"Maybe."

"Who was riding with him when they lynched Murphy?"

"Can't say."

"Can't or won't?"

"I told you, I wasn't here when it happened."

"No, but you're the foreman. You would've heard the whole story when you got back."

"I heard stories, but that's all they were, just stories."

"In these 'stories' you heard, who rode out with Coltrane to hang Sean Murphy?"

"All I'll say is it wasn't any of the working cowboys. There are three men Mr. Coltrane has to do work the cowboys can't or won't do. Maybe they were with him, but I don't know it for a fact."

"You mean gun hands. Men who burn down barns and shoot whoever they're told to shoot."

"Can't say."

"You're in this, Ed. Maybe you don't want to be, but you're in it. Take my advice, ride away. When I come for your boss, I'll take down anyone who gets in the way."

"I told you. I ride for the brand."

"So do I."

"Ride away yourself. This isn't your fight."

"Yes, it is. I represent the owners of the Rocking M, and I ride for another brand."

"What are you talking about?"

"I'm branded myself, Ed, with a star. I'm John Everett Sage, the Sheriff of Alta Vista County. I have work to do. After I get the Rocking M cattle home, I'm going to arrest your boss for murder and theft of private property."

Ed's mouth dropped open.

"Does Mr. Coltrane know who you are?"

"I expect so. If he doesn't know by now, he'll find out soon enough. Still, I'd appreciate it if you'd keep that bit of information to yourself."

Ed laid his reins over his saddle horn and rubbed his face with both gloved hands. When he picked up his reins, he looked at me, squinting.

"Well, hell, if that don't muddy the water. Alright, he won't hear it from me, but let me tell you one thing. You're drawing from a marked deck. You've upped the ante and the pot is full. You're playing for all the chips, but this is a rigged game. Mr. Coltrane don't ever lose."

"He's already lost. He just doesn't know it yet."

Ed leaned forward and started his horse trotting toward the camp. He turned to look at me over his shoulder.

"I wouldn't bet on it."

DAN ARNOLD

28.

Most of the families of the cowboys and ranchers had come to the camp under Haystack Rock for the usual get together at the end of the roundup.

The atmosphere wasn't as festive as usual. The news of Jimmy's death had been a sad reminder of how hard life can be. Many of the cowboys were riding nighthawk because the herd wouldn't be let go until the sale cattle were cut out the next morning.

Still, the children were playing and running around like wild Indians. They were under close supervision, to keep them from spooking the herd. Half a dozen musicians were doing their best to liven the atmosphere. The ladies had brought some home cooking which included pies, cakes and cookies. Ace and Henry were the center of the ladies attention and because the three of us were together, I was a lucky beneficiary as well. Among the men in camp, the mostly hidden and subtle application of alcohol was loosening things up. The Cross brothers were plenty loosened up and there was nothing subtle about it.

Ed signaled the musicians to stop playing for a moment. He stepped up on a bucket.

"Can I have your attention, please" Ed called out.

The din of conversation began to die down. A loud whistle jerked everyone to a stop. The crowd began to assemble in a circle facing where Ed stood on the box in front of the musicians.

"Shuddup. Cand ju she Baxter has shome, uhh, somethin' to shay?" Curt Cross slurred so badly, it was hard to understand him.

I was glad he'd whistled instead of firing his gun, which he held in his hand. Evidently he planned to use it to get everyone's attention if the whistle had failed. His drunken action would've endangered the crowd and might've spooked the herd.

"Thank you, Mr. Cross..."

"Nothin' uff it." Curt said, struggling to holster his gun.

"I want to take this opportunity to thank all of you for the hard work you put in today. You all know we lost a man. Jimmy Johnson was a good boy and a good cowboy. He'll be missed. Mr. Johnson, I'm sure I speak for everyone here when I say how sorry we are for your loss."

There was a murmur through the crowd and Ace bowed his head and nodded his acknowledgement of the sentiment.

"We branded over four hundred calves, of which two hundred and ten were bull calves, now steers. The total head count came to over a thousand head. We paint marked about four hundred to be sold, and they'll be moved to the holding pens in Buttercup, tomorrow. John and I have a tally of every critter here, and how many head per ranch are being sold. Mr Coltrane would like to say something about that. Mr. Coltrane, come on up."

I hadn't seen Jud Coltrane earlier. It seemed he was avoiding the limelight. After Ed stepped off the bucket, Coltrane stepped up.

"Thanks, Ed. I want to announce that I've negotiated the price for the sale of our beef. Let me introduce two gentlemen, Mr. Tom Guinn, and Mr. Leroy Lefever, cattle buyers from Denver."

The assembled crowd applauded politely.

"These gentlemen were bidding against each other, but soon decided to combine their efforts and keep the price down."

The crowd grumbled in disapproval.

"Now don't be discouraged. You should have more faith in me. These men are hard bargainers, but not as hard as me. I'm proud to announce, the price of beef has gone up. Ladies and gentlemen, we're getting four dollars and ten cents per hundred weight, on the hoof, delivered in Denver!"

The crowd didn't react. They were trying to figure out if it was good news or bad.

The cattle buyers looked at each other, then up at Coltrane.

"Folks, let me break it down for you. Those are prices as good as Chicago and there's no shipping cost. Our cattle here are very fat and healthy. A mature steer will probably weigh about a thousand pounds, some cows more. That means forty one dollars a head, more or less, on average. You can take that to the bank!"

Heads were nodding all around.

Until about 1885 the cattle market had been booming, with prices approaching eight dollars a hundred weight, and then it crashed.

The following winters had decimated many herds, but here the winters hadn't killed off many and the location with available shelter and hay production was ideal for raising healthy stock. Now the price of beef was recovering and the locals were in position to capitalize in the market. The timing was perfect. The range was overstocked and unless some cattle were sold, serious damage would be done.

Coltrane had done right by himself and his neighbors. The Rocking M stood to make about four thousand dollars. If the price held, we could do it again next year and every year after that.

Four thousand dollars was more than twice what I made in a year. It was a lot of money. I reminded myself it was money Coltrane had been planning to put in his own pocket. Money he would not let slip through his fingers if he could find a way to avoid it.

"I'll see to it everyone selling cattle gets the full price. We're moving the sale cattle to Buttercup tomorrow. Each ranch will have to provide a couple of cowboys for the drive down to Denver. That'll take a couple of days. I'll have your money for you by the end of the week. How does that sound?"

"Wahoo," someone yelled. The band struck up a tune and Coltrane stepped off the bucket, shaking hands as he worked his way through the crowd.

Ace was watching me as we stood together by our cook fire, so was Ed, from over by the band. I didn't figure this was the time or place to confront Coltrane. He was pretty popular with the crowd at the moment, and I had no idea where his gun thugs were.

That question was answered a moment later, when I turned and found myself staring across our cook fire at Snake Flanagan and his massive friend Higgins, as they emerged out of the darkness outside the camp.

"Howdy. I've been wondering where you boys were. I guess working cattle isn't something you enjoy."

RIDING FOR THE BRAND

Ace was in the process of pouring coffee into a cup. Henry was off somewhere with his friends. The Cross brothers were too drunk to stand, much less help. I figured Flanagan and Higgins had been waiting for a time when it was just Ace and me. Ace set the pot down and casually took a few steps off to one side, making sure we were now two targets instead of one, and he had room to move, if it came to a gun fight.

"Never did care much for cattle, amigo. Besides, we've been in Bear Creek running an errand for Mr. Coltrane." Snake said.

I was studying the situation, wondering if I could get them both if it came to gun play. They were pretty close together, but Snake was said to be fast. I didn't know how well Ace would do in a gun fight. I was praying it wouldn't happen. There was still a

345

crowd of people milling around behind us. If Flanagan and Higgins started firing, many people could be killed or injured and the herd would probably stampede.

What was it Ed had told me? He'd said something about three gunmen. So far I'd only met these two. Where was the third man?

Another figure stepped up beside me.

"Hey, John, the Rocking M has a hundred head in the herd being driven down to Denver on Tuesday. I was wondering, how many cowboys can you provide for the drive?" Ed Baxter asked.

I noticed he was standing off to my left, facing Snake and Higgins. Ace was on my right doing the same thing.

"I figured to hire a couple of hands tomorrow. Will two be enough?"

"Sure, that's fine." Ed was staring at Flanagan and Higgins. "Howdy, what brings you boys out here tonight?"

"None of your damned business, Baxter. Go take care of your cows. We're here to talk to Sage." Higgins said.

"Actually, whatever happens at this roundup is my business. This is a friendly get together we're having here tonight. I intend to keep it that way. State your business and be on your way."

"We don't take orders from you. We work for Jud Coltrane."

"Is there a problem here?" Buster asked, stepping into the firelight next to Ace.

That did it. Four against two were odds Snake didn't like. I saw it on his face. Higgins was still trying to figure it out.

"No, there's no problem. We just wanted to have a word with Mr. Sage here. We'll do it another time." Snake said.

"Uh uhh. Do it now." I said.

Snake sighed and looked up at Higgins. "Ok, show him what we brought, my friend."

Higgins grinned and reached inside his jacket.

I never meant to draw, but my gun was leveled at him before I thought about it.

"Whoa, John. Let the man show you what he has. There's no need for that" Snake said.

Higgins scowled at me as he slowly drew a folded sheet of paper out from a vest pocket. As he began to unfold it, I holstered my Colt.

"You say you represent the owners of the Rocking M. Well, they don't have no

348

claim, no more. This here's the deed from some feller named Kennemer." Higgins said, holding the sheet of paper up so I could see the writing. He tossed it into the flames. I was closest to the fire. I almost made a dive for it, but now was not a good time for a sudden move. No one moved.

"See? Poof, just like that, there's no record of any deed to Murphy."

I almost laughed. What was the old saying? Stupid is as stupid does.

"Where did you get that deed?"

"County Clerk's office, up at Bear Creek."

"I see. You rode up there, found the deed and tore it out of the deed records. Is that it?"

Higgins grinned and nodded.

"Had to ask for help. There's a bunch of deeds.

"Doesn't matter. It doesn't change the fact, just complicates the record. I'll bet you never looked in the indexes."

"The what?"

"Never mind. Burning the deed doesn't negate its validity."

Higgins looked at Flanagan for an explanation.

"He says burning the deed doesn't change anything."

"Yeah?" Higgins turned back to me. "Well I say you got no business here. The Murphy heirs don't own the Rocking M, and the cattle are all mavericks. If you take them off the range, you're a rustler."

"Is that what you say, or what your boss says?"

"It don't matter, Same thing."

I nodded.

"Yes, you're right. It is the same thing. It comes from the south end of a northbound bull."

Buster chuckled at that. Higgins' open-mouthed stare and sidelong glance at Flanagan showed his momentary confusion.

"You've been warned. You'd better haul your freight." He said

"Is that it then? Anything else?" I asked.

"Nope, that's it. You git."

"Well then, gentlemen, our business here is done. You have a nice evening."

"OK, amigo. We'll be seeing you." Snake said. He gestured to Higgins indicating they should leave.

When they were gone Ed turned to me.

"John, those men are hired guns. They intend to see you put under."

"They're not the first."

"Maybe not, but they mean to be the last."

I slapped him on the shoulder. Feigning more confidence than I felt, I smiled and said,

"Don't worry about it. So did the others."

THE ROCKING M –
CHANGES AND CHANCES

29.

I approached the ranch buildings with caution, mindful that Snake Flanagan and Higgins were gunning for me. This would be the logical place to jump me. Here, they could bushwhack me while I was alone, at any time of the day or night.

The situation brought into focus my promise to Lora.

Once again, I left Dusty tied to a cottonwood limb while I circled the buildings on foot. There was no sign anyone had been here since we rode out a couple of days ago. No horse or human tracks since the rain, anywhere I looked. Still, there might be someone hidden in the house or up in the loft of the barn.

Rifle in hand, from a corner of the barn I dashed across the yard to the back porch, where I flattened against the wall by the door. I'd almost expected to be caught in rifle fire from both the house and the barn.

Waiting for my heartbeat to slow and my breathing to return to normal, I scanned everything in sight and listened for any sound from inside. It was quiet and peaceful.

Birds flitted through the trees and a dragonfly buzzed through the yard. Otherwise, there was no movement.

When I pulled the back door open, nothing happened, and nothing was what I was hoping for. I stepped through the doorway and once again flattened against the wall. The room was empty, exactly as Old Bill and I had left it.

RIDING FOR THE BRAND

It was time to get cleaned up. There wasn't enough time to light the fire and heat water for a bath, so a cold bird bath would have to do. I stripped off my clothes and pumped water into the sink. I was glad it wasn't winter. Even without the stove being lit, the house was reasonably warm.

I hadn't shaved since I left Bear Creek, and without plenty of hot water, I wasn't going to attempt it now. At home we had hot and cold running water in our bath room, piped in directly from a wood fired water heater in the kitchen.

Thinking about it made me miss Lora and the kids more keenly than I had since finding this place. I reminded myself that everything I was doing down here was for the benefit of Jake and Sarah.

Thirty minutes later, I was dressed in in my suit, even the celluloid collar and tie, running a comb through my freshly washed hair. It felt wonderful. I was tired from working long days and a bit stiff from sleeping on the ground, but strangely refreshed in body and mind. I thanked God for that.

I walked out to where I'd left Dusty tied and watered him in the creek. There was still no sign of Buster and the saddle stock.

***

Riding down the hill from the entrance of the Rafter J, I was surprised at the number of people, buckboards and horses surrounding the house and outbuildings. It looked as though there was a wedding or party of some sort in progress. Were these people from the other farms and ranches that had come for Jimmy's burial? The thought hadn't occurred to me. I'd assumed I might be the only visitor.

I rode Dusty down to a corral beside a barn, tied him with a neck rope and unsaddled him. I was startled to see the four horses in the pen were the Rocking M saddle stock. Evidently Buster was here somewhere, stopping off on his way to the Rocking M.

Leaving the tack on a fence rail, I walked over to the house.

Several cowboys I'd met on the roundup greeted me as I approached, including Gabe Partridge and Ed Baxter. I shook hands with the latter two men.

"I figured ya'll would be back at the Bar C Bar." I said.

"We were. I understand you need hands to help drive the sale herd down to Denver. I'd like to be one of them." Gabe said.

"I'd appreciate the help, but won't it be a conflict for you? You ride for the Bar C Bar."

"Nope, I'm fixing to quit that outfit. I can't ride for somebody as low as Jud Coltrane. I'd rather ride the grub line."

"What do you mean by that?"

"I've seen his hired guns and I know what he uses them for. Everyone knows what he did to Sean Murphy. Left to his own devices, he'll take over the range, no matter who has to be hurt or killed. Then he'll ruin it. Some of us are sick of it. I'm not the first to quit him."

"I see. It just so happens the Rocking M is hiring. We'll need a couple of hands, not just for the drive to Denver, but to stay on and work the ranch. Can you shoe a horse?"

"Yes, sir, I can."

"Most cowboys want to rope and ride. They don't like to be set afoot. The rocking M is a small outfit and we're mostly fenced. How do you feel about that?"

"The wire is pretty much everywhere these days. I'd have a hard time finding another outfit that wasn't fenced. This is the wrong time of year to start looking."

"Are you willing to ride fence? Will you put up hay, and do whatever work needs doing?"

"Yes, sir."

Well then, I'd like to have you, if you'll ride for the brand."

"I might. What are you paying?"

I laughed. I like a man who gets to the point.

"For an experienced hand like you, we'll pay a dollar and a half per day and found. You know how it is, you'll work at least six days a week, but we'll pay for seven and we'll provide the saddle stock."

"Seems fair."

"We'll drive twice a year, once in the spring, to move some or all of the stock up into the high country, and again in the fall to bring them back down."

"Oh. I'd like that."

"Before you decide, I should tell you there's trouble coming. You know what's going on. You should know something else." I opened my suit coat showing the badge pinned to my waistcoat, "My name is John Everett Sage. I'm the County Sheriff."

Gabe shot a look at Ed, who nodded his affirmative.

"Holy smoke!"

"I intend to arrest Jud Coltrane for the murder of Sean Murphy."

"He has hired guns. I'm no gunfighter."

"I'm not asking you to fight. I just want you to know the next few days might get hairy. You'll be gone to Denver with the sale herd, but even that could be dicey. If you take the job, you'll start riding for the Rocking M as soon as you get back."

"No sir."

"Not interested, huh? I understand. It's why I told you the whole deal."

"No, what I mean is, if you'll have me, I'll start tomorrow. I'll be riding for the brand on the drive to Denver."

I slapped him on the shoulder and extended my hand.

"That's capital. We have a deal."

Ed watched us shake on it with some interest. As I walked away, he fell in beside me.

"Let me ask you this, John. You say you ride for the brand and you're the foreman for the Rocking M, but you're also the County Sheriff. How's that work?"

"It doesn't. I never knew anything about the ranch when I first rode in here. When I learned the ranch belonged to the Murphy heirs and Old Bill Kennemer, I figured someone should represent them at the roundup. I can't be the Sheriff and the foreman. My home is in Bear Creek. As the crow flies, that's more than fifteen miles from here."

"I expect you'll have to choose."

"I already have a job. I'm the Sheriff. The kids need to be in school. There's no school in Buttercup."

"Sounds like you need more than one man at the ranch."

"I sure do. The day to day operations have to be handled and one man can't do it by himself. I'm hoping Old Bill will look after things. The place is half his."

"I've never met him. Is he around?"

"Yep, around here somewhere. He's strange though. Likes to keep to himself, roams around. I don't think he's ever really settled anywhere."

"I'd sure like to meet him."

"I hope you get the chance. I can't go home until I work out some things with him."

"Will that be before or after you arrest my boss?"

"That's another problem. I can't go home without my prisoner."

"You think that's a problem? You'll be lucky to stay alive."

"I don't believe in luck, Ed. I believe God has a plan. I may not know exactly what

363

it is or what I'm supposed to do, but the plan is in place. I just need to trust Him and do my best to follow were He leads."

"Or die trying."

30.

On the front porch of the Johnson home, several men were engaged in conversation. It seemed most of the women were inside with Mrs. Johnson. At the top of the steps I was met by Henry Burke, the store keeper in Buttercup.

"Howdy, Mr. Sa... er, John."

"Relax, Mr. Burke, after today, everyone will know who I am. Did you send that telegram for me?"

"Sure did. I was hoping I'd see you here." Henry reached inside his coat and handed me a folded telegram. "I waited for the reply, just like you asked. Imagine that, a telegram from the governor himself."

I gave the telegram a quick look.

The governor simply said he had no objection to me arresting any suspect I deemed necessary. This was his way of saying that although Jud Coltrane's wealthy and influential family might object or even interfere, he would not.

It didn't really matter to me much anymore, but when I'd composed the telegram I was aware of the possible complications for both the governor and myself. The telegram was intended to give him notice so he could make his own plans.

If he'd sent a reply that I should not proceed with my plan to arrest Jud Coltrane, I would've done it anyway, but at least I'd know what to expect. I had no desire to make an enemy of the governor, but justice had to be served—no matter the cost to me personally.

"I was going to bring it out to you at Haystack Rock, last night, but Lida needed me to help her cook and gather some things for the Johnsons. It's just terrible news about young Jimmy."

"It is indeed. Thank you for this, Mr. Burke."

"Something else you might be interested to know. While I was in Bear Creek, I saw them gunslingers that Coltrane has doing his dirty work."

"How many men were there?"

"I just seen that big fellow Higgins and the one they call Snake."

"What were they up to?"

"I don't know. They were on the square by the courthouse."

I nodded my understanding.

"Thanks again, Mr. Burke. Do I owe you anything?"

"Nope. We're square."

I looked around at the little knots of people.

"I must say, I'm surprised by the turnout here. I hadn't expected so many people to be in attendance."

"The Johnsons are good folks. Most everybody is, except that polecat Coltrane. It's natural for friends and neighbors to gather around someone who's hurting."

"I had no idea something this bad would happen on the roundup."

"It happens more than you might expect. Last year Mike Waters, he rides for the Flying W. He got bucked off a horse and dragged. Busted up pretty bad. Part of his head was stove in. We all thought he'd die. After a week or so he woke up. He gets around pretty good these days. Sorta moody and mean mouthed, kinda forgetful too, but he can still work. We all took care of his missus and the kids, for a spell. You know, just till he was back on his feet."

RIDING FOR THE BRAND

"Is Jud Coltrane here?"

"Humph! Not likely. He hates the ranchers that haven't buckled under. Ace Johnson has been nothing to him but a thorn in his side. Now, you've come along. No, I don't believe we'll see Mr. Coltrane today."

Ace walked out on the porch. He nodded at me, and then spoke up loud enough for everyone to hear.

"I want to thank all of you for coming out here for Jimmy's funeral. We're taking him over to the family plot now...Again, thanks for coming."

There was movement behind him and five men emerged carrying a coffin made of pine planks. Ace took hold of the sixth rope handle. The others carrying the box were Ace's remaining sons.

We all stepped aside as the coffin went by, then fell in around and behind Mrs.

Johnson and the three girls as they went down the stairs. I saw Buster walking beside Katie. She took his hand. It appeared some of the women around Mrs. Johnson noticed this. No doubt it would be cause for gossip.

It was a sad parade that hiked over a small foot bridge and up the side of a hill to the little family cemetery. Inside the decorative fence were two graves with limestone markers and a freshly dug hole. I noted the names on the markers. The dates indicated they were both young children, one an infant girl and the other a three year old boy. Jimmy wasn't the first child the Johnson's had lost, maybe not the last.

Two ropes had been placed across the open grave. Four cowboys held the ropes taut as the coffin was lowered onto them, then they gently let the coffin down into the grave. When the ropes had been removed, everyone stood by in silent respect, the men removed their hats.

Seeing there was no preacher in attendance, I felt I should speak up.

"If I may, I'd like to say a word."

Ace nodded. His red rimmed eyes indicating he was too choked up to speak.

"Mr. and Mrs. Johnson, thank you for sharing your son with me, these last few days. Like you, I'm proud to have known him. He was a fine young man and a good hand.

Mrs. Johnson, yesterday you reminded me of the words from Job. The scriptures record those words. 'Naked came I from my mother's womb and naked shall I return there. The Lord gave, and the LORD hath taken away; blessed be the name of the Lord'.

And, I'm reminded of these words of comfort from our Lord, recorded in the book of John; 'Let not your heart be troubled: ye believe in God, believe also in me. In my Father's house are many mansions: if it were not so, I would have told you. I go to prepare a place for you. And, if I go and prepare a place for you, I will come again, and receive you unto myself; that where I am, there ye may be also'.

I believe it's certain we'll see Jimmy again one day, on the other side."

Mrs. Johnson attempted to smile through her tears, her gracious nod acknowledging her understanding and gratitude.

Suddenly, a beautiful tenor voice began to sing:

"In the sweet by and by, we shall meet on that beautiful shore:

In the sweet by and by, we shall meet on that beautiful shore.

There's a land that is fairer than day.
And by faith we can see it afar;

For the Father waits over the way

to prepare us a dwelling place there."

Others joined in, one by one. As we began the refrain again, the song swelled.

"In the sweet by and by, we shall meet on that beautiful shore:

In the sweet by and by, we shall meet on that beautiful shore.

We shall sing on that beautiful shore.

The melodious songs of the blessed;

And our spirits shall sorrow no more,

Not a sigh for the blessing of rest.

In the sweet by and by, we shall meet on that beautiful shore:

In the sweet by and by, we shall meet on that beautiful shore.

To our bountiful Father above,

We will offer our tribute of praise

For the glorious gift of His love

And the blessings that hallow our days."

Now, with bittersweet joy, we were all singing.

"In the sweet by and by, we shall meet on that beautiful shore:

In the sweet by and by, we shall meet on that beautiful shore."

As the song faded away, I couldn't help looking at Buster in appreciation. His strong clear voice had come as a complete surprise. His timing had been superb. Katie was looking at him with something akin to awe.

"Amen." Ace said, pulling on his hat. "Folks, please go on up to the house. These kind ladies have brought enough food to feed an army."

RIDING FOR THE BRAND

Everyone began to wander back toward the house, leaving the Johnsons to have a moment alone by the grave.

I looked back to see Ace Johnson filling in the grave, with his family gathered around him.

DAN ARNOLD

31.

Immediately following the funeral, I saddled Dusty and rode back to the Rocking M.

Buster told me he'd bring the saddle horses over whenever he could get away from the Johnson ranch. I didn't expect to see him soon. He'd spend as much time with Katie as possible.

Now that we were fenced, there was only one way back to the Murphy ranch from the Rafter J. Approaching the headquarters of the Rocking M with a great deal of caution was becoming a habit. As soon as I closed the gate behind me, I started a wide arc toward Yellow Butte, figuring to come up behind the ranch buildings from a different direction for a change.

This time, I didn't dismount. I rode slowly along the face of the mesa, weaving quietly in and out of the chaparral and fallen rock, with my rifle in my hand.

I stopped frequently scanning for tracks and listening to the sounds of the afternoon. Everything seemed normal. When I was within a couple of hundred yards of the buildings I turned toward the creek, crossed it and rode along the far edge, screened from view by the pussy willows.

I came to a place where I could just see the house over the tops of the willows. I sat and watched, until I was sure there was no movement there.

Turning Dusty, I loped up the hill behind me. This brought me out in the open, about two hundred and twenty five yards from the house. I figured if someone was waiting to ambush me they might try a shot. The gamble was on whether they'd be able to hit a moving rider at that distance. If there was a shot, I'd slap spurs to Dusty and get away from there.

No shot was taken, so I turned toward the house, crossed the creek and rode up into the front yard. Again, everything was quiet. I dismounted and led Dusty around the house and back to the corrals by the barn. When he was unsaddled I turned him out in his pen where he could get water from the trough, climbed up into the loft and forked some hay down for him. Anticipating the arrival of the rest of the Rocking M saddle stock, I did the same in the adjoining pen.

Once in the house, I set my rifle by the door, lit the stove, and took my coat and hat off.

I'd just poured some hot coffee when I heard the sound of horses outside. That would be Buster bringing in the saddle stock. I poured an extra cup for him and walked out on the back porch to greet him.

"Freeze, Sage."

The pressure of the shotgun muzzle against my cheek stopped my hand from fully bringing my Colt out of the holster. Out of the corner of my eye, looking down the double barrels of the ten gauge, I saw the smiling face of Higgins.

Snake Flanagan was sitting his horse in the yard about fifteen feet away, leading Higgins mount. He had his Colt pointed directly at me. It was a good plan, so audacious I fell for it. Higgins had dismounted and snuck up to the house and was waiting for me on the back porch when Snake brought their horses into the yard. I hadn't figured on them doing something so bold.

That was no excuse for my carelessness. Lora made me promise to come home safe. I'd failed to keep my promise. Now I wouldn't be coming home at all.

"Put your hands up high, amigo. Slow, now. That's good." Snake said.

As I began to raise my hands, Higgins eased around behind me. He never let the muzzle of the shotgun break contact with my head. The slightest movement or an accidental increase in the pressure on the trigger would send particles of what had been my head all over the yard.

Snake slid off his horse, carefully, never taking his eyes off me or his aim off my heart.

He took a couple of steps back and to the side, standing about twenty feet away.

"I told you we would face each other soon. This is that day. I want to know something. They say you shot Rawlins down in a stand up gun fight on the street in Bear Creek. It takes a real man to do a thing like that, look another man in the eyes from a few feet away and reach for your gun.

Are you such a man? I don't' think you are. I am. Do you want to try?"

I was planning on it. No matter how they killed me, I had to try.

"I see it in your eyes, amigo. Understand this, you will die now. Even if you could get me, Higgins will blow you to kingdom come. Nothing can change that. You should say your prayers."

"I'm prayed up. Are you planning to shoot me down while I'm standing on the porch with my hands in the air?"

Snake was good. He never took his eyes off me.

"No, I don't want to look up at you. Come out into the yard."

"Are you ready, Higgins?" He asked.

"Itchin' to get him."

Higgins increased the pressure on the back of my head, following me as I slowly stepped down into the yard.

"That's close enough, amigo."

He made a movement with his head, indicating Higgins should move away from me.

"Come on Snake. Let me send this lawman straight to hell, without a head."

"That is not what we talked about, remember? You will give him both barrels in a moment. First, I get to shoot him down and then you blow him to pieces."

Higgins cursed, but he eased away from me maybe fifteen feet, over near the porch rail, keeping the shotgun trained on my head.

Any second now, whether I employed the most delicate or the fastest move, I would be dead before I knew what hit me.

"You don't give a man much of a chance do you?"

"I know it's not fair, but it's the only chance you get today. You get the chance to choose which way you'll die."

Snake holstered his Colt and raised his hands.

"I will count to…"

As I drew and fired, Higgins made a noise and the shotgun roared.

Snake's bullet slammed into the .38 hideout revolver in the holster under my arm, helping me spin toward Higgins.

He was falling, with part of his head gone.

384

I spun all the way around to fire at Snake again, but he was down.

I stood there in shock. How was I still alive?

DAN ARNOLD

32.

After the sudden gunfire, the silence made me think I might be deaf. I felt frozen in place. I took a deep breath, more of a gasp really. I realized I'd been holding my breath. Hearing the sudden intake of air, I discovered I wasn't deaf.

When I could move, I more or less staggered over to where Snake Flanagan lay sprawled in the dirt.

My bullet had taken him just under his nose, ruining his face and killing him instantly.

I realized I still had my Colt in my hand. The trauma was taking a toll, I'd begun shaking, making it difficult to replace the spent shell and then holster my gun.

What had happened here?

I pulled out my .38. Flanagan's bullet had hit the edge of the back strap in the grip and glanced away, tearing away a chunk of the wood from the grip. My ribs were bruised from the impact, but nothing was broken. My left arm had still been up and out to the side, so the ricocheting bullet hadn't hit it.

Flanagan was fast, probably much faster than me, but his aim had been thrown off by my sudden action.

I walked over and looked at what remained of Higgins.

Nearly half his head and his hat were gone, just gone. It wasn't from the shotgun blast I'd heard. The wound looked more like his head had exploded. Someone had shot him, probably with a big bore rifle. I listened and scanned the area, but I was the only living person anywhere near this place. A rifle requires a clear line of sight. From a distance

388

the trees and brush outside the yard would've blocked anyone's view, much less a shot. I never heard the sound of a rifle shot.

I managed to get to the bench on the porch, nearly collapsing onto it. I sat there for several minutes staring out into the yard.

The flies were already buzzing around the corpses.

I was alive and they were dead. How could this be?

I remembered everything that happened in that second when Flanagan began to count. I reached, seeing Flanagan's hand drop for his gun, impossibly fast. We both fired at virtually the same time. Wait. Higgins made a noise just as I started for my gun. What was the sound? Something like a bat hitting a baseball. The shotgun roared as I was firing my Colt. Three guns all firing at virtually the same time. The cacophony of gunfire had been deafening. The buckshot from the ten guage must've passed directly over my head.

As I was thinking these thoughts, the sound of approaching horses reached my ears.

Ducking into the house, I grabbed my rifle and knelt by a window.

Buster rode into the yard with his rifle in his hands. He was ponying the four saddle horses behind him. First, he saw the two riderless horses standing in the yard. The sight of two dead bodies made him pull up quick.

"John, are you here?"

"I'm inside. Are you alone?"

"Sure am. Do you need help?"

I opened the door and walked out onto the porch with my rifle at the ready.

Seeing me, Buster turned and slid his rifle into the scabbard.

RIDING FOR THE BRAND

"Are you, OK?"

"Somehow, I guess I have you to thank for it."

Buster dismounted.

"How's that?"

"I figure you shot Higgins over there."

Buster pulled the lead ropes off his saddle horn.

"Me? I never shot anybody. I was just closing the gate when I heard gunfire over this way. I came as fast as I could, figuring you were in trouble. Looks like I was right. I see you handled it."

He turned away, leading the horses over to the empty corral. He tied his mount to a post then turned the Rocking M stock out into the pen. After closing the gate, he laid the halters and lead ropes over a fence rail.

When he returned I was again sitting on the bench by the back door.

"Are you sure you're OK, John?"

"I can't figure it. They had me dead to rights. I shot Flanagan. Who shot Higgins?"

Buster surveyed the yard and the surrounding area.

"I don't know what you're talking about. You're all alone here. Looks like you got both of them."

"No. I couldn't have done it…"

"Do you have any whiskey? I think we could both use a drink."

"Huh? Whisky? No, I don't have any."

"How about coffee? I'll make it."

"There's a fresh pot on the stove. I poured you a cup, but it's probably cold by now."

"Stay there, John. You're not making any sense."

RIDING FOR THE BRAND

Buster walked into the house. When he came back out he handed me a cup. Maybe the hot coffee would help clear my head.

I sat on the bench. Buster leaned against a porch post with his back to the scene in the yard. We drank our coffee in silence.

DAN ARNOLD

33.

I sat on the bench by the back door and concluded God had somehow spared my life. It reminded me I had much to be thankful for.

I was still sitting on the bench and staring out into the yard, when Old Bill Kennemer just materialized from behind some chaparral. I thought I was seeing things.

Buster seeing my expression, spun around reaching for his pistol.

Old Bill held up a hand.

"Hold on there, sonny. I come in peace. I reckon there's been enough gun talk for one day."

It dawned on me then. Seeing Old Bill cradling that Creedmoor rifle in the crook of his arm brought everything into focus. It was his shot that saved me. His shot—by God's grace.

"Who might you be?" Buster asked him.

"I might be one of the owners of this spread. Who might you be, sonny?"

"My name's Buford Cavender. My friends call me Buster."

"Well then, Buster, ain't ya gonna offer an old man a cup of coffee?"

Buster looked at me. Seeing my smile, he proceeded into the house.

I stood up and walked out to meet Old Bill. As we shook hands I thanked him for saving my life and added, "Your mighty quiet in those moccasins. We didn't hear you coming."

"Pays to be careful. You should try it. You got yourself bushwhacked. That was too close.

I couldn't see the big man once he was on the porch. I seen him sneaking in, but I figured you probably seen him too. I kept my rifle on the little guy. I was some surprised when you walked out in the yard with that big feller holding a scattergun on you. I had to rethink my target. Damned near too late."

"Where were you? I can't imagine how you were able to see anything at all."

He pointed a thumb over his shoulder.

"Top of the mesa. Hell of a view from up there."

I looked toward the top of Yellow Butte.

"Bill, that has to be over half a mile from here."

He nodded.

"I calculate it's about eight hundred and fifty yards, about a third of that in elevation. Tricky shooting. Good thing it ain't windy."

I stared at him. How could an old man even see that distance? He only had one chance to make the shot and he had to put the bullet exactly where he did, or Higgins would've killed me.

"That's the most amazing shot I've ever heard of."

Old Bill shrugged.

"I was using a new-fangled rifle scope I picked up in San Francisco. I've had some practice with it, but not at any such range. A shot like that could make a fella kinda nervous, but I had the strangest feeling, peaceful and real focused like. Say, things are some changed around here."

Buster came out with a cup in one hand and the pot in the other.

Old Bill held up a hand, stopping him on the porch.

"Sonny, do you expect me to drink my coffee standing in the yard with these dead men?"

"Uhhhh...No, sir."

"Well then, put the coffee on the table, then go out and bring in my horse. He's waiting a couple hundred yards northeast of here. Big Appaloosa, white blanket with black spots big as silver dollars, ya can't miss him."

Buster looked at me again.

I just chuckled.

***

Old Bill and I were sitting at the table when Buster came in.

"I've got to head on back to the home place, John. I have half a dozen broncs to feed and water."

"Ok, Buster. Thanks for bringing in our saddle string."

"What do you plan to do with those dead men out in the yard?"

Before I could answer, Old Bill spoke up.

"Well, sonny, I reckon they'd be mighty poor poker players and easy to beat if we was pitchin' horseshoes. We'll probably have to bury em somewhere. Don't ya think?" He asked.

Buster gritted his teeth and looked up at the ceiling, shaking his head.

"They were riding Bar C Bar horses. Someone will come looking for them."

I sat up.

"That's a good thought, Buster. I believe I'll take the bodies and the horses back to the Bar C Bar tomorrow morning. That way we won't have to bury them."

RIDING FOR THE BRAND

"Won't that be dangerous?"

"Goes with the job."

"After you left the Rafter J, there was talk about you being the County Sheriff. Is that true?"

"It is."

Old Bill's eye brows shot up for a second. This was news to him as well.

"Is it true you're going after Jud Coltrane?" Buster asked.

"I have to. He murdered Sean Murphy and stole property from this ranch."

"You can't do it alone. What I mean is, if you need a deputy…"

"That's a fine offer. I might just take you up on it, one of these days. I expect you're making better money as a wrangler and all around bronc fighter."

"Two years ago, at the rodeo in Bear Creek, I scored higher than Tom Horn.

401

Course it was mostly just luck of the draw. I drew a better bronc. I'm just saying, if you need any help…"

"I hear you, Buster. I know you came riding in here when you heard gunfire. It takes a brave man to do that. I won't forget. It means a lot to me. Much obliged."

We walked outside with Buster. He'd tied the Appaloosa to a post with the thin mecate Old Bill used as a neck rope. The horse's fancy bridle with the silver spade bit was hanging on the saddle horn.

As Buster rode out, Old Bill turned to me and said,

"Lawman, huh? What's your plan?"

34.

My plan was to arrest Coltrane for murder. He was guilty and everyone knew it, but I was up against a nearly insurmountable obstacle. The only witnesses to the crime were the men who had committed it.

I looked at the two dead men where they lay in the yard.

"Here's the problem as I see it, four men lynched Sean Murphy, these two, Jud Coltrane, and another man who is unknown to me. There were no other witnesses. When we shot Higgins and Flanagan here, we killed half of those who were involved."

"If you ask me, that's not a problem. It's a job half finished." Old Bill said.

"I need to arrest Jud Coltrane and the other man for murder, but when it comes to trial, it means one will have to testify against the other. It seldom happens, because that kind of testimony is self-incriminating."

"Then we catch the third man and make him talk. I can make him squeal like a pig. He'll give up Coltrane, just before he dies." He made a twisting motion with a closed hand, as though holding a knife.

I ignored Old Bill's bloodthirsty suggestion.

"I don't know who or where the third man is. I'll have to get somebody to tell me. Maybe someone at the Bar C Bar knows something. It's unlikely Jud Coltrane will talk."

Old Bill spat on the ground.

"Leave Coltrane to me."

"Who made you judge, jury and executioner? Would Sean want that? It's time for law and order, not retribution. I know you were his partner, Bill, but this is a matter for the law."

"So you say. Like I asked, lawman—what's your plan?"

"Let's drag the bodies into the barn. In the morning we'll throw them over the horses they rode in on. The sale cattle are being driven to Denver, tomorrow. I plan to stop in Buttercup on my way to Coltrane's spread and ask a few questions before the herd moves out. Then I'll drop off the horses and the corpses at the Bar C Bar.

"Was that big fella the one you tussled with here?"

"Yep, his name was Higgins. He stole the original deed you provided to Murphy and then he burned it. In the County Clerk's office there are still references to the deed, but no actual deed. We'll need to replace it. There's no paper here. When we get to Buttercup,

405

would you write out a replacement deed? I can help with the wording."

"Course, glad to do it."

"From there, I'd like you to shadow my every move, staying out of sight, watching my back. No one else could do it as well as you can. What do you say?"

Old Bill nodded. Looking at the bodies in the yard, he said, "Let's start with the big man. Grab a foot."

***

After we closed the barn door, Old Bill said, "Saddle a horse. There's something I want to show you."

Dusty had been working nearly all day, so I chose Shangaloo for the ride.

We headed west, more or less following Buttercup Creek where it cut through the mesas at the edge of the mountains. Shortly, we began to climb, leaving the lower grassland behind.

After a time Old Bill said, "We're on the far end of my half section now. This is the route you'll use to move the herd up into the high country."

He led us down a steep mountainside through pine forest and aspens, to the edge of a fairly deep pool where another, smaller creek merged into Buttercup Creek.

Following his lead, I dismounted beside the pool.

We were in a narrow canyon strewn with boulders. The way we'd ridden down the mountain was the only access to this pool. The surrounding mountainsides were covered with rockslides and thick forest.

Looking around, I said, "It's a beautiful spot, Bill. Thanks for bringing me up here."

"Found it when I was prospecting."

While we watered the horses, Bill told me why we were there.

"I told you I named this creek Buttercup to discourage cattlemen, them not wanting their cattle to eat Buttercups. That's true enough, but only part of the story. This spot, right here, is the real Buttercup." He pointed at the pool.

Setting his rifle against a tree trunk he reached into a vest pocket. He turned and tossed me something a little smaller than a hen's egg, only much heavier. It was a gold nugget. One of the biggest I'd ever seen.

"I pulled that out of here, evening before last. I first found this pool about thirty years ago. Filed a mining claim. Over the years I've stopped by on occasion, and she ain't never failed me. The mother lode is up in these mountains somewhere, but there's

408

plenty of gold right here. Been washed down over time, I reckon. If a feller had a mind to, he could pan, up and down these streams, maybe set up a sluice box. Might get rich."

"Is that what you're going to do?"

Old Bill took off his sombrero and let it hang down his back. His long white hair fairly sparkled in the last rays of mountain sunlight this late in the day. He squinted at me, grinning, his tanned face becoming etched with lines and wrinkles.

"Me? I made my fortune in California in '49. Held onto it and made some more since then. I've got more money than I know what to do with."

"Are you ready to settle down? The ranch needs somebody to run it."

Old bill stroked his stained mustache.

"The years have gone by like flying birds or passing storms. Now, I'm long in the

409

tooth. I've gotten where, like an old dog, I'm happy sitting by a good fire, or laying out in the sunshine."

"It's perfect then. I have to go back to Bear Creek, and do my job as the County Sheriff. You stay here and run the ranch."

Old Bill produced his pipe and tobacco pouch. He tamped tobacco into the pipe, and then struck a match. When he was satisfied with the way the pipe drew, he glanced over at me.

"I don't have many years left. There's places I ain't never been. Did you know down in Mexico and all the way down into Argentina, there're ancient cities built of stone, just ruins now, where thousands of people used to live? Some even high in the mountains. I sure would like to see those."

"What are you saying?"

410

He blew smoke out his nose, and tossed the burnt match into the pool.

"I can't stay here and just fade away." He made a forward motion with his pipe. "I have to keep moving."

"Then why are you showing me this place?"

"The Rocking M belongs to Sean's kids. All of it. I believe you'll take care of em and see they get educated. That takes money. Your being a lawman is dangerous and we both know you ain't a careful man." He winked at me. "Sooner or later, you'll have to quit it. Sooner, I hope. Those kids need a father."

"Bill, are you trying to give me your claim?"

He jabbed the stem of his pipe at me.

"Ranching ain't certain, ya know. There're bad years. There has to be something in the bank."

"Bill, I don't want you to go, and I don't want your money."

"When we draw up the new deed, I mean to give you my half section and the mining claim. In return, I want your promise—your word of honor, you'll take care of Sean's children as if they were your own."

"My wife and I intend to. I only came down here to determine whether Jake and Sarah had kinfolks who might have a right to raise them."

"Stuck your foot in it didn't you?" He asked, settling his rifle back in the crook of his arm

"Both feet, up to my knees, but I'll slog through it."

He nodded.

"I reckon so. I've been watching you, John. You'll do. Shake my hand and we'll have a deal."

DAN ARNOLD

35.

In the wee hours of the morning, once we'd accomplished the grizzly task of slinging and securing the bodies of the two dead gunmen on their horses, Old Bill and I set off for Buttercup. It was very cold, I figured near freezing.

As we rode along, each of us leading one of the Bar C Bar horses, I reflected on Old Bill's generosity.

Before we left the pool in Buttercup Creek, I'd tried to give the gold nugget back to him. He held up his hand and said, "For all you know that may be the last of it. What if there's no more gold in this pool, or in the creeks? You might have a claim on nothing. You'd better hang onto it. It might be all you ever get. 'Sides, you don't even know if that nugget really came out of this pool, do you?"

415

"I'll take your word for it."

We mounted our horses.

As I started following him back up the mountainside, without looking back, he said, "To me, a man's word is worth more than gold."

***

We rode into Buttercup just after seven thirty in the morning. There were more horses and men than I'd previously seen in the hamlet. Seven or eight cowboys had assembled over at the livestock pens. Everyone was bundled up in heavy coats and chaps.

"Looks like they're about ready to pull out." Old Bill said.

We must've been a sight, leading those Bar C Bar horses with dead men across the saddles. All eyes were on us.

RIDING FOR THE BRAND

As we dismounted in front of the general store, Gabe and the others trotted their horses across the bridge to meet us.

"Morning, Boss." Gabe said. "What's all this about?"

"Gabe, meet R.W. Kennemer. He's half owner of the Rocking M."

As they shook hands, I said to Bill, "I should've told you. I'm hiring men to work the ranch."

"None of my business. Never was." He said.

"Who're they?" Gabe asked, with a jerk of his thumb toward the corpses.

"A fella named Higgins and Snake Flanagan. They tried to bushwhack me at the Rocking M. It didn't work out like they planned."

The cowboys all looked at each other with expressions of surprise, horror or general distaste.

"Jud Coltrane's hired guns." Gabe said. "These are Bar C Bar horses."

"Is Ed Baxter around? I'd like to ask him some questions."

"No, sir, he's at the Bar C Bar. He told me I should ramrod this outfit on the drive to Denver." Gabe said. He looked around at the cowboys. "Everyone agreed."

"OK. Let me ask ya'll. When Sean Murphy was lynched as a rustler, did any of you see who was in the necktie party?"

The cowboys either shook their heads or said nothing.

"Gabe, you were riding for the Bar C Bar. Do you know who did it?"

"Well, Mr. Coltrane is proud to say he did it. I figure these two dead men were with

418

him, but I was miles away, over to the east of the tracks with a couple other hands. We didn't hear about it till we got back to headquarters, several hours after it happened. That's all I know. You should ask Ed Baxter. He's the foreman."

I nodded my understanding.

"Alright, thanks. You men be careful on the drive to Denver."

I turned and walked into the general store, with Old Bill on my heels.

"Morning, Sheriff. What can I do for you gentlemen today?" Mr Burke asked, as I closed the door. He was looking at Old Bill with some curiosity.

"Morning, Mr. Burke. Would you happen to be a notary?"

"Why, sure, Postmaster, notary, you name it."

419

"We'll need paper and pen. This gentleman is R.W. Kennemer. He was Sean Murphy's partner. Say howdy to Mr. Burke, Bill."

As they shook hands, Old Bill said, "I understand you and your Missus buried Sean and his wife. I'm mighty obliged to you."

Lida Burke chose that moment to walk in from their living space behind the store.

"Yumpin yiminy! Are you really "Old Bill" Kennemer? By golly, we've heard of you. Sean spoke of you that often, he did. Such stories he told."

"He could tell a tale. How'd you folks come to know where to find his body?" Old Bill asked.

"The foreman of the Bar C Bar came in and told us about the hanging and how to get to where it happened."

"Ed Baxter?"

"That's right. Now, what kind of paper do you gentlemen need?"

"We'll need a couple of pieces of decent writing paper. We're drawing up a replacement deed from Mr. Kennemer to Sean Murphy. That big gunman Higgins stole the original from the County Clerk's office. We'll put it back on record."

"That, and another deed from me to the Sheriff, here." Old Bill added.

Mr. Burke disappeared behind a counter and returned with a pen, an ink well and several sheets of paper.

"Here you go. It's called velum. Best we have, Penny a page, though."

"We'll need at least three." Old Bill said. "John, you'll have to write out the deeds. I don't know the lingo."

"Yep. They're called warranty deeds—I'll do the writing, but you'll have to read them before you sign anything."

"Then you'd better write slow and neat. My eyes aren't what they used to be." Old Bill said, with a wink.

Once the deeds were drawn up, read and signed, Mr. Burke notarized them. When it was time to go, Old Bill asked me to wait outside. He had something he wanted to talk about with the Burkes.

Outside, I looked across the creek and watched the drag riders pushing the tail end of the sale herd south, until they disappeared out of sight.

36.

I found the headquarters of the Bar C Bar right where Mr. Burke said it would be. He hadn't mentioned the house was a huge clapboard affair on the top of a hill. The two story house was raised up off the ground a good eight feet, with a wide porch on the front. I imagined the view from up there would be spectacular. The house was whitewashed and the roof was covered with dark gray shingles, as were all the barns and outbuildings.

While the overall effect was clean, bright and tidy, there was something austere, even harsh about the hard lines and cold appearance of the house. There were no trees or shrubs, all had been cleared away. Not even a hanging fern or potted plant was to be seen, nothing to soften the effect of the high, box like structure.

There were horses in the whitewashed pens and I could hear a blacksmith hammering away on a piece of iron. Smoke rose from the chimney of the cookhouse. The door and the windows of the bunkhouse were open, and the curtains billowed slightly in the gentle breeze. Evidently it was being aired out prior to being buttoned up all winter.

A couple of hands saw me approaching and waited with evident curiosity to see who I was and what I was packing in on the horses I had in tow.

In one of the pens I passed were half a dozen big harness horses. Two were branded with the Rocking M. In the next pen were broodmares, some with the same mark.

I pulled up where the two men stood waiting. I recognized them. I'd first met them in the bar in Buttercup. They'd avoided my company at the roundup.

"Howdy, boys, do you remember me?"

"Uh huh. You ride for the Rocking M. What do you want here? Say, are those dead men?" The older one gulped.

"These are your horses and the dead men worked for your boss. I'm just returning Bar C Bar property."

"Uhhh, we don't know anything about that?"

"Go fetch your boss."

"Which one?"

"Mr. Coltrane, who do you think?"

"He ain't here."

"Who's in charge here?"

"Our foreman, Ed Baxter. He's up at the big house. I'll go fetch him.

"Wait. You boys take charge of these horses. I'll go up to the house."

Before they could answer, I dropped the reins of the Bar C Bar horses, turned Dusty and loped him up the hill toward the house.

When I arrived at the bottom of the stairs leading up to the porch, I dismounted and left Dusty ground tied.

As I started up the stairs, a loud voice boomed, "Stop right there."

Ed Baxter stood at the top looking down at me.

"You don't need to come up here, Sheriff Sage. Mr. Coltrane isn't here. He's gone to Denver to handle the sale of the cattle."

I started slowly up the stairs.

"You won't mind if I take a look."

"I do mind. Are you calling me a liar?" His wide stance and the way his hand hovered near his gun indicated he meant to fight.

I stopped.

"Is this it then, Ed? Are you standing against me?"

"I reckon so."

I held my hands up.

"I'm not going to shoot with you, Ed. I'm here to make an arrest."

Ed drew his gun and pointed it at me.

"No. you're not going to take another step. I'll give you the chance to turn around and leave. Otherwise I'll shoot you down where you stand."

"That's not going to happen. Justice will be served, but I'm not going to shoot you and you're not going to shoot me. Nobody dies here today."

427

"You're about to find out different."

He cocked his pistol.

"Before you start shooting, I'd like to say something."

He nodded slowly.

"Alright, say your piece."

I stretched my arms higher.

"You asked me if I was calling you a liar. Well, yes, Ed. I sure am.

Ed suddenly spun to his left and as he fell, I heard the sound of the distant Creedmoor.

I walked the rest of the way up the stairs. On the porch, Ed was kneeling in a rapidly spreading pool of blood. I kicked the gun out of his right hand as he attempted to point it at me. His left arm was nearly severed just above the elbow.

If I didn't get some pressure or a tourniquet on it within a minute or two he would bleed out. I stepped over to the open front door and ripped down the curtains framing the glass panel. I wrapped one of the curtains around his arm and used the curtain rod to twist it tight.

He screamed at the pain, breaking out in a sweat.

"Sorry, Ed. You're under arrest for the murder of Sean Murphy. You slipped up, telling me there were three men who would do whatever Jud Coltrane paid them to do. The first two, Snake and Higgins, are dead. You're the third man. You lied when you told me you weren't there when Sean Murphy was lynched. You told the Burkes exactly where you hung him."

Through gritted teeth Ed said, "I'm foreman of the Bar C Bar. Mr. Coltrane decided it was time to get rid of Murphy, and like I told you, I ride for the brand."

DAN ARNOLD

37.

Stretching my arms up was the signal telling Old Bill to take the shot. I'd made him promise not to kill anyone, just wing them. He helped me get Ed into the house, where we made him comfortable on a couch.

I sent Old Bill to Bear Creek to fetch deputies and on the way, ask Lida Burke to come help me with Ed. I instructed Old Bill to send a telegram, while he was in Bear Creek, to United States Marshal Maxwell Warren, in Denver. The telegram asked Max to arrest Jud Coltrane on charges of murder and theft, and then oversee the sale of the cattle. The proceeds of the sale were to be sent back with Gabe.

Later that afternoon, Buckskin Charlie and Old Bill reached us a good half hour before the buckboard driven by a deputy.

431

DAN ARNOLD

***

While the cowboys were burying Snake Flanagan and Higgins, a search of the buildings and pens at the Bar C Bar produced most of the stolen horses and equipment from the Rocking M. It was all inventoried and catalogued to be introduced as evidence at the trials of Jud Coltrane and Ed Baxter. When the trial ended, everything would be returned to the Rocking M.

That same evening, Buckskin Charlie and the deputy took Ed Baxter back to Bear Creek in the buckboard, but not before Buckskin Charlie had a chance to shoot Old Bill's Creedmoore rifle. After shattering bottles at two hundred and fifty, then five hundred yards, he said it was the best rifle he'd ever fired. Old Bill was impressed Charlie could be so accurate with a rifle he'd never fired before.

RIDING FOR THE BRAND

Old Bill and I rode back to the Rocking M.

He didn't stay. He didn't even dismount.

He shook my hand with both of his, turned his Appaloosa, and headed out to "look around".

***

It had been four days since Old Bill rode away. By now, I figured he was probably headed south, somewhere between Buttercup, Colorado and Argentina.

I was almost desperate to go home to Lora and the children, but I had more work to do.

I'd ridden around to each of the ranches that sent cattle to Denver, telling them the story, and letting them know as soon as Gabe returned, their money would be held for them at the general store. Mr. Burke had agreed to hold the money; he had the only safe in Buttercup.

"Now I'll be postmaster, notary, store keeper and banker. Look at me, momma, I'm coming up in the world." He said.

Lida Burke just smiled and patted him on the back.

***

When he returned from Denver, Gabe and I sat at the table and counted the money, dividing it up into packets for the different ranches. I didn't know what to do with the money belonging to the Bar C Bar. I decided to leave it with the rest, on deposit with Mr. Burke.

Early on a Saturday morning, Gabe and I rode into Buttercup with the money. It was cold, the sky heavy with clouds threatening snowfall. As we traveled, Gabe told me I could hire as many hands as we

434

would need, from those still working at the Bar C Bar.

"Pick two good men, no more. Somebody has to stay on to run that ranch. The money from the cattle they sold belongs to the brand. There's plenty enough to pay the hands and I expect Jud Coltrane will need some of it for attorneys to defend him when he goes on trial in Denver." I said.

"I'll tell you one thing. Denver is getting plumb civilized. When we brought in the herd there were a lot of people watching. I reckon they don't get to see many cattle drives these days. Coltrane was waiting for us at the stockyard. You should've seen the look on his face when that U.S. Marshal arrested him."

"I imagine he was some put out."

"Yep."

"Probably embarrassed.

"Uh huh.

"He say anything?"

"Nope."

"Smart."

***

At the general store, the Burkes greeted us with warmth. When I told them Old Bill had left the country, they told me what he'd done for them. Henry Burke was mighty excited. He opened the safe and handed us two heavy coins.

"Mr. Kennemer told us he was grateful for what we done for the Murphys. What with buryin' them and all. Said he wanted to have proper headstones made for them. He gave me a fifty dollar gold eagle to pay for the stones. Fifty dollars! I never seen a gold eagle before. Then he gave us another one, to pay for shipping or whatever. The whole bill for headstones with engraving and shipping from Denver wouldn't come to more than twenty five dollars. I told him so. He just grinned, slapped me on the shoulder and walked out, smoking his pipe. Can you believe it?"

"Yes, Mr. Burke. I sure can."

We'd just seen the gold coins and the money from the cattle sale locked away in the safe, when three men walked into the general store.

The man out front was dressed in a dark gray suit and tie with a matching bowler hat. He had the look of a prosperous gentleman. His manner suggested he was used to being treated with respect.

I glanced at Gabe. He'd seen what I had. The other two men had the look of trouble.

They were dressed similarly to the gentleman, but gun belts were in evidence and they moved with the cautious conservation of effort common to fighting men.

Gabe eased toward the door, thinking to get behind them, but one of them saw his intent and turned to block him.

The other gunny focused his attention on me, where I was standing near the back of the store with my hands crossed in front of my belt buckle.

"Good morning, you must be the storekeeper." The gentleman said, addressing Mr. Burke.

"Good morning sir. I'm Henry Burke and this is my wife, Lida Burke. This is our store."

The gentleman removed his hat.

"How do you do? My name is Nordwick. I'm the legal representative of Jud Coltrane, the owner of the Bar C Bar ranch."

The other two men never took their eyes off either Gabe or me. They weren't about to remove their hats. If they were going to remove anything, it would be their guns from the holsters.

"How do you do? How can we be of service, Mr. Nordwick?"

"I was given to understand John Everett Sage, the County Sheriff, was in occupancy at the Rocking M ranch. Is that correct?"

Mr. Burke glanced at me.

"Yes sir. Last I heard."

"We were just there—and he was not. Have you any idea where we might be able to find him?"

Once again, Mr. Burke glanced at me. I nodded back at him.

"Good morning, Mr. Nordwick, I'm Sheriff Sage."

Tturning his head, the man shifted his gaze to me, looking me over.

"I see. While you don't have the appearance I'd expected, let me say your reputation precedes you, sir."

I neither moved nor answered.

"Mr. Nordwick turned his back to the Burkes, as though they no longer existed.

He looked at his men, at Gabe, then back to me. You could've cut the tension in the room with a knife.

"I see we understand each other, so I'll get straight to the point. I have in my possession a restraining order against you, Sheriff Sage. In light of your well known proclivity for violence, Judge Walters in Denver issued the order. You are not to be seen anywhere in the vicinity of the Bar C Bar ranch. Further, these gentlemen are agents of the Pinkerton Agency. They will conduct a search of the Rocking M ranch to determine whether any of the livestock or other property of Mr. Coltrane's ranch is now in your possession. Do you understand what I'm telling you?"

I smiled at him.

"Yes, Mr. Nordwick. I understand what you said. There's nothing on the Rocking M for you to see. You should be aware my department conducted a search of the Bar C Bar. We found considerable stolen livestock and other property belonging to the Rocking M ranch on the premises. It's all still there and it better stay there, as its evidence of Mr. Coltrane's criminal activity. A full inventory was taken, which will be presented at the trial.

May I see the restraining order and some proof you actually represent Jud Coltrane?"

I uncrossed my hands, resting my fingertips together.

The Pinkertons moved their hands closer to their guns.

Mr. Nordwick gently removed a folded sheet of paper from inside his jacket and tossed it at my feet.

I locked eyes with the man.

"Pick it up and hand it to me, Nordwick, or whatever your name is."

He sniffed and sneered, "Pick it up yourself."

"Yumpin yimminy! Stop it, by golly! I won't have this in my store." Lida Burke said, as she came bustling from behind the counter.

I watched the two Pinkerton agents. They looked to their boss.

With some effort, Lida bent and picked up the document, handing it to me.

"If you men are gonna fight, take it outside, don'tcha know!"

I looked over the restraining order. After a moment, I relaxed, chuckling.

"Thank you, Mrs. Burke. There's no need for a fight. This seems to be a legitimate court order. There won't be any trouble here. I intend to fully comply with the restraining order."

Nordwick's eyebrows shot up, expressing his surprise.

"That's it? You're just going to ride away?"

"Of course, I have no grievance with you, Mr. Nordwick. My business in the area is concluded.

The funds from the sale of Bar C Bar cattle have been deposited with the Burkes. If you're able to satisfy any concerns they may have as to your right to represent Mr. Coltrane, they'll let you have the money."

Mr. Burke blinked several times, attempting to formulate a response.

I nodded toward Gabe.

"This is Gabe Partridge, the foreman for the Rocking M. We're going back to the ranch now. You and your friends from the Pinkerton Agency are welcome to ride along."

Mr. Nordwick opened his mouth, but nothing came out.

I started walking toward the door, the Pinkerton men stepping aside.

"If you'd prefer to come later, that's fine, but I won't be there. Gabe will be in charge. I'm on my way back to Bear Creek. I'm going home."

HOME AGAIN,

38.

I stopped Dusty on the sloping side of the mesa just above the bridge over Bear Creek. I often stopped here to enjoy the view of the County seat of Alta Vista County, the city of Bear Creek, Colorado.

The highest point in the city was the courthouse at the top of the hill. The other tallest structures were the church steeples. The city was rapidly spreading out, so rapidly now, only the streets in the central business district, and the closest adjoining, were paved with bricks. In the spring, telephone lines were to be strung from the city, all the way down to Denver.

At the bottom of the hill upon which the city was built, on the western edge of the organized blocks and neighborhoods, right next to Bear Creek, sat our beautiful whitewashed, two story house on thirty five acres. The place I now called home.

From my elevated position on the road, I saw the harness horses out in the meadow and I could just make out the children playing in the front yard.

I'd brought a surprise with me, but it was somewhat spoiled by the fact I'd been spotted on the bridge as I crossed over the creek. The children had alerted Lora and all three of them were waiting for me at the front gate.

I jumped off Dusty and wrapped Lora up, kissing her boldly, to the delight of the children.

RIDING FOR THE BRAND

I knelt down, Jake and Sarah rushed in for a hug.

"John Wesley Tucker! You said you'd be gone for just a few days, and it's been more than a week. Well, at least you aren't all shot up." Lora said. "You aren't hurt are you?"

"No ma'am. I'm healthy as a horse. Speaking of which, look what I brought with me."

I brought the horse around from Dusty's off side.

Jacob's eyes lit up with recognition.

"Shangaloo. Look, sissy, it's Shongaloo. Do you remember Shongaloo?".

Sarah shrugged, uninterested. She probably didn't remember the horse.

"I found him down around Yellow Butte. He was your dad's horse wasn't he, Jake."

Jake nodded silently, a somber expression on his face.

"Well, he's your horse now, son."

Jake's mouth dropped open, his eyes wide with wonder and obvious delight.

Lora searched my face. Seeing my smile and nod, she understood the situation. She scooped up Sarah, holding her tight. "He doesn't know how to ride, John." she said.

"He'll learn. I'll teach him. Would you like that, Jake?"

"Yes sir!"

"Good, I'll give you your first lesson this afternoon. Right now, you can start by leading him down to the barn. Here, take this lead rope—now don't look at him, look where you're going. Atta boy, I'll open the pasture gate. Just follow me down to the barn."

***

RIDING FOR THE BRAND

Buckskin Charley was more than eager to give me back my seat behind the desk in in the courthouse.

He brought me up to speed on the condition of Ed Baxter.

"Doc had to take his arm off, John. He was afraid of gangrene. There was too much broken bone and tissue damage. Baxter will have to live the rest of his life with only one arm. Hell of a thing to happen to a top hand."

I nodded.

"I hate to hear it. Then again, he brought it on himself.

He'll probably hang for the murder of Sean Murphy and all the other crimes he committed while he was riding for Jud Coltrane."

Charlie nodded his agreement with my statement, and said, "Baxter's arraignment is set for Monday. Doc thinks he'll be strong enough by then. He's weak as a kitten right now, but he can walk well enough. By Monday, he should be able to handle the stairs.

We're holding him on the lynching charge. Do you want to add some more charges to it?"

"Yep, he should also be charged with attempted murder of a peace officer, horse theft and maybe even negligent homicide— Mrs. Murphy died shortly after learning her husband was lynched. Probably can't make that stick, though. I still get mad thinking about Jake and Sarah leaving their mother's body and walking barefoot all the way here."

"I understand how you feel, John, but it may be hard to prove. Much of what you've told me is just your word against his. You say he pulled a gun on you, and the horses and equipment were found on Coltrane's ranch, but you can't prove Ed Baxter had anything to do with stealing from the Rocking M."

"He was the foreman of the Bar C Bar. The Rocking M horses and equipment didn't just magically appear on the property without his knowledge."

"I expect when it comes down to a jury decision, knowing is one thing, doing is another"

"Charlie, you're a pretty good Chief Deputy, but I swear, you should've been an attorney."

"Maybe, but you know I'm right."

I took a long, deep breath and let it out slowly.

"Yep, I reckon you are, at that."

"Do you still plan to charge him with those things?"

"The only thing he confessed was the lynching."

"Did you ask him how the horses and equipment were stolen from the Rocking M?"

I shook my head.

"There wasn't occasion to ask many questions. He was holding a gun on me at the time. After he was shot, he wasn't in any shape to talk about much of anything."

"He can talk now."

I gave it some thought. Ed Baxter wasn't likely to offer any information, not if it would only serve to further incriminate himself. What if I had something to offer in return? Maybe we could make some sort of deal.

"You know, Charlie, what you said before about it just being my word against his, was true. This whole thing was Jud Coltrane's doing. He's the one who should face the worst consequences. He could go free if there isn't anyone to testify against him. Ed Baxter is the only one who can do it.

Ed is an honorable man. He only went along with Coltrane's plans because he was riding for the brand. That's no longer the case. Maybe we can make a deal."

"That's what I was thinking. Coltrane will have the best lawyers money can buy. I'd hate to see Baxter swing, while Coltrane goes free."

"That won't happen. Not if I can help it. I believe I'll have a word with our prisoner."

DAN ARNOLD

39.

I found Ed Baxter sitting on one of the bunks in cell four. He had the space to himself because of his injury. He was reading a book lying open in his lap. He turned the pages with his right hand. His left sleeve was tied in a knot below the stump of his severed arm.

"Howdy, Ed, how are you?" I asked.

"Howdy, John. Or should I say, Sheriff Sage?"

"You can call me John. I'd like to think we could still be friends."

"Why? I nearly killed you."

"You didn't try it out of hate. You didn't even want to do it. You thought you were doing what your job demanded."

He nodded.

"That's right. I ride for the brand."

"You did, but you don't anymore. Coltrane is locked up in Denver. He'll only come back here to stand trial for the murder of Sean Murphy. You understand, you no longer ride for the Bar C Bar?"

"No, I guess I don't. Not anymore. Not since this." He indicated his injury.

"I'm sorry about that."

"It could've been worse. I could be dead. I guess I will be, in a couple of weeks."

"Listen, about that, I'd like to help you out."

"What, you're going to let me go?"

"No. You'll have to stand trial, but you don't have to hang. I think I can help keep you alive. You'll have to do some time, but you'll be out in in a few years."

"How does that help me? I figure I'm better off dead."

456

"Why, because of the arm?"

He nodded silently.

"Come on, Ed. You're a top hand in anybody's outfit. Sure, you lost an arm, but you can still rope and ride."

"I don't know, maybe." He shrugged and then he focused on me. "I didn't lose my gun arm."

"And you didn't lose your savvy. You know cattle, horses and men, better than most cowboys ever will."

"Is there some point to this visit, John?"

"You're too good a man to end up swinging from the wrong end of a short rope. If you testify against Coltrane, you won't hang for the murder of Sean Murphy— Coltrane will."

"How's that?"

"You told me once you never believed Sean Murphy stole cattle from the Bar C Bar. Is that still true?"

"Murphy was a good man. All our cattle ran together on the range. Murphy didn't rustle any cattle. I'm sure of it. I would've known if he did.

"Did you have something personal against Murphy?"

"No, nothing personal. Like I said, he was a good man."

"Was it your idea to lynch him?"

"No, I was against it. I tried to talk Mr. Coltrane out of doing it."

"That's my point, Ed. You never set out to kill Murphy. No reason you should hang for something Coltrane cooked up. He'll try to pin the whole thing on you. Are you going to let him get away with murdering both Murphy and you?"

Ed closed his eyes and twisted his neck as he considered his options.

"I'll let you think about it, Ed. Coltrane didn't deserve a good man like you. He's a bad man and he has no respect for you. He'll throw you away as quick as he would a used corn husk in the outhouse. He has no honor"

I walked away.

***

"I sure am glad to see you, John." Tom said. "Things are moving fast on the completion of the orphanage. The county commissioners approved a budget three days ago. They expect to see it staffed as soon as possible. Here, take a look at the newspaper." He pushed it across his desk toward me.

I was relieved to see there was no direct mention of me or my department. It seems my being away had broken the cycle of abuse normally heaped on us.

The headline was about the saw mill coming to North Fork. Below the fold, was a simple story about the establishment of the orphanage.

County orphanage to open its doors

This reporter has learned that Alta Vista County will soon have a facility for the care of orphaned children. A special meeting of the Commissioner's Court approved a budget and the immediate hiring of staff for the orphanage. The facility, which will house and feed as many as two dozen children, is situated in the town of North Fork on twenty five acres donated to the county by a local business person.

In related news, construction of a new church has commenced on land adjacent to the orphanage. This reporter has learned plans for starting a school in that community are also being discussed.

***

"Well, Tom, I call that progress."

Tom grinned at me.

"Yep, it sure is. The new preacher up there stopped by here to tell me about the plans for the school. At first, it will meet in the church house. He says he figures they'll have at least twenty five children the very first day."

"A saw mill, a new church, a school and an orphanage all happening at once, aint that something? Who would've ever figured North Fork would become civilized so fast?"

"Times are changing everywhere. It's getting hard to keep up."

"Yep, it sure is."

"So, how are you feeling, John? You sure look healthy. Did you learn anything useful down around Yellow Butte?

I grinned back at him.

"Yes, Tom, I sure did. Lora and I are going to adopt Jake and Sarah."

"Capital, that's just capital. I'm so happy for you. I can't wait to tell Becky."

"I imagine Lora's already told her."

"Well let's all get together tonight and celebrate. What do you say?"

"I say that sounds capital."

***

We make our plans, but God alone knows what a day may bring forth. I had no idea my trip to Yellow Butte would be the thing that put me right. I haven't had a nightmare since the day I rode down there.

The snow will soon be falling, another year starting not long after.

462

I hope this letter finds you feeling well, Mother, and enjoying the weather in California. Lora sends her love, as do I.

May God bless you and keep you.

I remain lovingly your son,

John

****

RIDING FOR THE BRAND

Turn the page for an Excerpt from:

YELLOW HORSE

SAGE COUNTRY

Book Four

An excerpt from:

YELLOW HORSE

SAGE COUNTRY

Book Four

By Dan Arnold

Jim Scroggins was a careful man. He prided himself on it. Trying to ambush the Indian in this high country was not the sort of thing a careful man would do. On the other hand, crossing Zeb Fletcher was even more dangerous.

Scroggins figured he'd have a little look around and go back to camp empty handed. Fletcher would be angry, but it was a risk he'd have to take.

From up here on the edge of the mesa he could see for miles. If the Indian was moving around below him somewhere he would be easy to spot. The thing was the savage might not be below him. He could be up on the mesa with him.

He cussed to himself. He should've thought of it before now. The sneaky bastard was here and somewhere close.

Scroggins cocked his pistol, listening. Nothing moved, except a flight of crows far off in the distance.

The blow came as a complete surprise, knocking his pistol out of his hand, now broken at the wrist.

He reached across his body to pull his knife, but another blow from the rifle stock slammed the wind out of him and sent him toppling over the edge of the cliff. He bounced off a couple of boulders before landing in a heap forty feet below, dazed and barely able to see.

RIDING FOR THE BRAND

***

Bending over the white man where he lay sprawled on the rocks at the base of the cliff, Yellow Horse observed two things. The man's body was broken, but he was still alive.

One eye was open watching Yellow Horse, the other eye destroyed by the crushed bones surrounding it.

"You damned injun. You've done for me." He said, through broken teeth.

"Not yet." Yellow Horse said. "First you will tell me where the woman is."

"No I won't. I aint tellin' you nothin'."

Yellow Horse nodded and began gathering small twigs and leaves from the ground. He placed them in a pile and widened his search, returning with larger sticks, which he placed next to the pile of smaller material.

"What are you doing?" The man asked.

"I'll make a fire. Nights get cold this high up."

Yellow Horse walked away. He was gone longer this time. When he returned he carried limbs nearly as thick as his arms, broken off from dead piñon and mesquite trees.

"Where is the woman?"

The man slowly shook his head.

"By now, the shock has worn off. The pain is setting in. I won't let you faint. You are hurt badly, but not fatally. Although many bones are broken, you are not paralyzed. Even the smallest movement will be horribly painful. You can't stand, probably can't crawl. In time you would starve or freeze to death here in these rocks, but not tonight.

Tonight we will talk. Tell me where the woman is."

"You go to hell."

Yellow Horse sighed and began building the fire.

When he'd arranged the loose leaves and twigs as tinder and built a small box around it with other twigs, he popped a match and lit it.

As the flames began to consume the twigs he added larger ones to it, then sticks. Now the fire was burning well, without any visible smoke. He remained squatted down facing the injured man on the other side of the fire.

"It's getting dark. Tell me where the woman is."

"No."

Yellow Horse stood and walked over to the white man.

"Unless you tell me, I will hurt you."

"Go on, do it. I'll never tell."

"You will. I'm going to burn you until you do."

The man closed his eyes, shaking his head.

Yellow Horse bent and grabbed one of the man's feet, yanking his leg straight.

The man screamed and nearly fainted, breaking out in a sweat.

"Where is the woman?"

The man was panting for breath

"Why do you care?"

Yellow Horse pulled on the man's boot, ignoring the screams, until he pulled it all the way off. There was no sock. The exposed foot was pale, nearly white, like the belly of a fish.

Returning to the fire, he squatted and set the boot down beside him. He waited until the man was breathing normally again.

"She is weak, can't survive here without help."

"What's it to you?"

Yellow Horse pulled a stick about as thick as his thumb out of the fire. He stood and blew on the smoldering end until it glowed, cherry red.

He walked back over to the injured man, grabbing the exposed foot.

He blew on the stick again.

"No, don't do it. It aint Christian."

"No, it aint."

"Wait, wait. Aieeegh!"

Yellow Horse barely wrinkled his nose at the smell of burning flesh. Dropping the foot, he turned back to the fire and squatted again.

He watched the white man where he lay whimpering. Once he'd settled down enough to hear and understand, Yellow Horse answered his question.

"I know her. She is a good woman. What you call a Christian, Not like you and me,"

Pulling another stick from the fire he blew on it and said, "We can do this all night. Tell me now. Where is she?"

***

RIDING FOR THE BRAND

A note from the author

Thank you for reading Riding For The Brand. I would love to hear from you. You can contact me at my website ~ www.danielbanks-books.com   where you will find a list of all my books, or follow me on Goodreads~ www.goodreads.com/author/show/10798086. Daniel_Roland_Banks

I hope you had as much fun reading this book as I had writing it. If you liked it please tell a friend - or better yet, tell the world by writing a book review on the book's page on Amazon, or on Goodreads.com.

Even a few short sentences are helpful. As an independently published author, I don't have a marketing department behind me. I only have you, the reader.

So please spread the word!

How do you write a review?

It's easy, just say...

Why you liked the book? What was your favorite part? Which characters were most interesting to you? Did you learn anything new or thought-provoking? Would you like to read another book by this author? You can look at other reviews to get an idea of what you might want to write.

Go to the Amazon or Goodreads link, click on the "write a customer review" button and type in your review.

And, to make it a little more fun, if you write a review, e-mail me and I'll return a note and an excerpt from one of my works in progress, maybe even a free e-book. Thanks again.

All the best,

About the Author

I've led a colorful life, fueling my imagination for telling stories set in the American West.

I was born in Bakersfield, California and abandoned by my parents in Seattle, Washington. After living in the foster care system for some years, I was eventually adopted. I've lived in Idaho, Washington, California, Virginia, and now make my home in Texas. My wife, Lora, and I have four grown children, of whom we are justifiably proud, not because we were such good parents but because God is good.

I've written several novels and an illustrated book on the training of horses, in addition to authoring and/or contributing to numerous technical manuals and articles in various publications and periodicals.

As a horse trainer and clinician (I trained performance horses for twenty five years), I had occasion to travel extensively and I've been blessed to have worked with a variety of horses and people in amazing circumstances and locations.

I've herded cattle in Texas, chased kangaroos on horseback through the Australian Outback, guided pack-trips into the high Sierras and the Colorado Rockies, conditioned and trained thoroughbred race horses, galloped a warmblood on the bank of a canal surveyed by George Washington, and spent uncounted, delightful hours breaking bread with unique characters in diverse parts of the world.

At one (brief) point I was one of the 3% of fine visual artists who earned their

12

entire income from sales of their art. I'm a painter, sculptor and writer.

Under the name Daniel Roland Banks I write contemporary detective thrillers. I'm a member of American Christian Fiction Writers and Western Writers of America.

My contemporary detective thriller, ANGELS & IMPERFECTIONS, was selected as a finalist in the Christian Fiction category in the 2015 Reader's Favorites International Book Award contest.

In 2013, after 40+ years of searching, I found and got reacquainted with my half-brother and a host of relatives from my mother's side of the family.

I can't sing or dance, but I'd like to think I'm considered an engaging public speaker, an accomplished horseman and an excellent judge of single malt Scotch.

DAN ARNOLD